WRANGLED BY THE
WATCHFUL COWBOY

SAGE VALLEY RANCH ROMANCE BOOK 3

TAMIE DEAREN

WRANGLED BY THE WATCHFUL COWBOY

To all my friends who struggle against the odds

"*I* probably shouldn't say this…"

"That's never stopped you before, has it?" Jessica Powell smiled at the sheepish expression on her grandmother's face.

"I get a new white hair every time I speak my mind." Sharon Buchanan laughed and shook her head, pointing at her curls—mostly salt, with a bit of pepper. "Obviously, I have no ability to hold my tongue."

As the kettle whistled, Jess rose from the table and put a hand on her grandmother's shoulder. "Stay here, Nanna. I'll get the hot chocolate. I'm excited you have your special mix, even though it's summer."

"I like to turn up the air conditioner so I can drink it all year." Nanna cleared her throat. "As I was saying, I'm glad you dumped Parker."

"Actually, he did the dumping," Jess said, "but I'd been thinking about it."

"Well, I say good riddance. He barely touched the

dinner I cooked when you brought him to meet us. He turned up his nose as if our food was too countrified for him."

"Don't take it personally. He's a vegan, so he couldn't eat your chicken-fried steak. That's why he always brings food with him." Jess put a third cup of cocoa mix into each mug and added hot water.

"Vegan, huh? I had plenty of vegetables. He didn't eat those either."

"Yes, but you season everything with bacon. That's a no-no for vegans."

"No bacon?" Nanna wrinkled her nose as she accepted the cup of hot chocolate.

"No meat of any kind or milk or cheese or eggs or honey." Jess rejoined her grandmother at the small kitchen table, idly stirring her cocoa with a spoon.

"I don't think I'd want to go on living if I couldn't eat those things. Did he try to turn you into a vegan? Is that why you broke up with him?"

Jess blew on her cocoa and took a sip, relishing the delicious rich chocolate. "I told you, *he* broke up with *me*."

Nanna scrunched her brows as if she had a hard time accepting this information. "Why? You're about as perfect as a girl could be. Beautiful. Smart. Barrel-racing champion."

"You're a bit prejudiced, Nanna, but thanks for that." Jess warmed under her grandma's approval. "He didn't really know about the barrel racing. I haven't done it since I transferred to UNT Dallas."

"You didn't tell him?"

"Trust me, he wouldn't have been impressed. He didn't even like my cowboy boots."

"You gave up your boots for Parker?"

"I didn't wear them around Parker. Honestly, I think his mother pressured him to break off the engagement. The Browns are big socialites in Dallas, and I wasn't from a rich family or polished enough to play one." Jess gripped her mug, irritated that the rejection still bothered her. "I think he only cared about my looks. He was always warning me I'd get fat if I ate too much."

This information sent Nanna's eyes into a slow roll. "Well, that proves it! I knew I was right about him. He was way too snobby." She lifted her mug, pausing before she drank. "Did you know he told Bucky he couldn't imagine people paying money to stay out here in the middle of nowhere?"

Jess felt guilty, hating that her sweet Grandpa Bucky—otherwise known as Peter Buchanan—had gotten his feelings hurt. She swallowed a spoonful of cocoa, feeling even more relieved that she no longer sported Parker's two-carat diamond on her finger. She'd been so enamored with him, but she now realized the attraction was purely physical.

"Honestly, Nanna, I don't even think I was in love with him." She glanced at her grandmother, whose expression softened, giving an encouraging nod. "I was just in love with the idea of him. One thing's for sure, I was never going to be good enough for him."

"Pish-posh! He wouldn't know the perfect girl if you hit him in the face. And maybe you should've."

"Nanna!"

"I won't apologize. I'm just glad you dumped him."

"But I—"

"You'll find the right guy, if you look in the right places."

"Well, I'm not looking." Jess bobbed her chin to emphasize her determination. "I've sworn off guys altogether, at least until after I graduate next May."

"I think that's wise." Nanna paused, clearing her throat. "Unless the right guy happens to come along. Then, you should make an exception."

Jess sipped her cocoa, contemplating her response, in light of her grandmother's suspicious behavior. "Nick said I shouldn't get in a rebound relationship."

"Since when are any of your brothers experts on romance?" Nanna grinned behind her mug and took another swallow.

"Zander and Cohen always keep their mouths shut. It's only Nick who has to put in his two cents on every decision I make. I told him to mind his own business. But in this case, I think he's right."

"I don't know." Nanna tilted her head, as if the matter were of utmost importance. "You and Parker broke up four months ago."

The problem was she didn't trust herself anymore. "I don't need a guy, to be happy."

"*Darn tootin'* you don't!" Nanna's mug slammed onto the wood table. Luckily it was almost empty. "You're strong, like all the Clark women," she declared, using her mother's maiden name.

"So you agree I don't need a man?"

"Of course, you don't need one." She paused until she had Jessica's full attention. "But if you find the right man, you'll *want* one. And we Clark women always get what we want."

Despite Nanna's playful wink, Jess knew she meant what she said.

"I'll keep that in mind, but I'm not in a hurry."

"You don't have to hurry. But you also shouldn't throw away a perfect opportunity."

"What are you talking about?" Jess shot Nanna a narrow-eyed glare.

"All I'm saying is you deserve someone who'll treat you like a queen. Someone like my Bucky." Nanna reached across the table to pat Jessica's hand, her expression the picture of innocence. "Have you considered dating someone from home? A nice country boy? Maybe someone you went to school with?"

"Sage Valley High is a small school." Jess tried to guess where her grandma's conversation was headed. "There was no one I liked."

"No one?" Nanna carefully smoothed and folded her paper napkin, her eyes averted. "What about Cord Dennison?"

Jessica's heart sped up at the mention of her closest brother's best friend, but she kept her expression carefully neutral. She'd been secretly in love with the hunky boy for as long as she could remember, writing page after page of "Mrs. Cord Dennison" and "Jessica Dennison" in the private notebook she'd kept hidden under her mattress. But he'd left for college before she started high school. "What about Cord?"

"Didn't you have a thing for him?"

How does she know? I don't remember telling her.

"I might've had a little crush on him when I was in seventh grade and he was a senior. But he left Sage Valley nine years ago and hasn't been back." With her cheeks burning, Jess studied the flowers on her mug. "What difference does it make, anyway? Nick told me Cord's at a big-shot software firm in New York. I won't see him again unless he's the best man at Nick's wedding someday. And let's face it, that's probably never going to happen."

"Oh, I think you may run into him sooner than you think."

Jess jerked her gaze to Nanna, but the dinging timer drew her grandmother's attention. She rose to retrieve a pan from the oven. "Are you sure you can't stay and eat a couple of fresh biscuits?"

"No, I already ate a protein bar for breakfast."

Nanna tsked her disapproval. "That's not enough to get you through a morning of hard work."

Jess ignored her scolding, though she was probably right. But thoughts of Cord had taken her appetite away, so she gave up on finishing her cocoa. "What were you saying about Cord? Is he back in Sage Valley?"

Nanna placed her cup in the sink and turned around, leaning back on the counter. "He came home to spend some time with his dad before he passed."

A violent shiver shook her body, putting herself in

Cord's place. "I would've done the same thing, I think. I'd have gone up to Oklahoma to be with Mom and Dad."

"Let's pray that doesn't happen," said Nanna. "Cord's father passed within two months of his diagnosis. Now his mom's staying with his sister, Caroline, and Cord's putting the ranch on the market."

"Cord didn't go back to his job in New York?" Feeling guilty, Jess struggled to hide her mounting excitement. *I can't be happy Cord's home under such awful circumstances.*

"He's still doing his work, but he does it on his computer, somehow. He's with a new company. Some outfit called Phantom Enterprises."

"*Wow*. Don't you know who that is, Nanna? They're like the biggest tech company in the country." Jess took one last sip of her cocoa and rinsed her mug out.

"Bucky and I don't exactly keep up with new stuff." Nanna swept her hand around the kitchen, which looked exactly the same as Jessica's childhood memories. "Cord came out to the ranch the week after the funeral and talked to Bucky and me for two hours. He seemed to want an excuse to hang around, and we gave him one."

"What do you mean?"

"We hired him." Nanna continued her explanation as she opened the dishwasher and loaded it. "As Cord puts it, he's going to bring Sage Valley Ranch into the twenty-first century. He's revamping our entire computer system—the accounting, the webpage, the payroll software… everything. And he promised to teach us how to keep it going when he's gone."

"That's nice of him." Jess knew they couldn't be paying him much.

"To be honest, we're counting on him to get us back in the black." Nanna loaded the last plate and shut the dishwasher, turning to face Jess. "Cord's doing some kind of profit and loss analysis on the ranch. We've been running half empty the past few years, even in the summer, and Bucky had to take out an operating loan. If we don't turn things around, we'll have to close the doors."

"Shut down Sage Valley Ranch?" Jess jumped to her feet and marched to stand nose to nose with her grandmother. "Why didn't you tell me things were tight, Nanna? Listen to me… I'm working free this summer. I absolutely insist."

Nanna's finger wagged in Jessica's face. "This is exactly why Bucky and I didn't tell you. We knew you'd throw a fit about being paid. But the truth is we really need you. I had to bribe your mother with one of my antique quilts to let you spend the summer here instead of with them in Oklahoma."

"She traded me for an old blanket. I see what I'm really worth," Jess teased.

"I'm counting on you to lead the trail rides. Cord saved us a lot of money, staffing the summer positions with volunteers." Nanna bent to check the contents of the oven. "Unfortunately, none of them know much about horses."

"What are they good for?" In Jessica's opinion, nothing else was important.

"Lots of other stuff. He put his head together with Charlotte, and they came up with some creative ideas. Two girls are leading daily outdoor yoga and workout classes. Cord has a couple of the guys in charge of water sports." With a clean sponge, Nanna wiped her already spotless counters. "He's also set up daily activities aimed at elementary-aged kids, to give parents a chance to go off on their own."

"That sounds pretty good," Jess admitted. Jess liked Charlotte, or *Charlie* as she liked to be called, who was in charge of guest relations at the ranch.

"He's already got us booked solid for the summer. I think we'll be out of the red in no time, although Cord's still worried about the cattle production end of things."

Jessica's mind churned. "I'll let you pay me at the end of the summer, but only if Sage Valley is making a profit."

"It's a deal," Nanna said. "Cord's dropping by this morning."

"He is?" Jess peeled her tongue from the roof of her suddenly parched mouth. She wasn't ready to face her childhood crush. Her hand rose to touch her hair, pulled up in a hasty bun. She hadn't even bothered to put on makeup.

I'm probably worried for nothing. He can't possibly be as cute as the boy from my seventh-grade memories. No one in real life has eyes that blue or shoulders that broad.

"When is he coming?"

Before Nanna could answer, the doorknob rattled, sending Jessica's stomach into her throat. She whipped around as the door opened. A long, boot-clad leg entered, followed by another. Her eyes traveled upward, past narrow hips and the muscles straining against a black t-shirt, to a strong jaw with a short growth of beard and a full-lipped mouth that set hers to watering. This was not the charming boy of her childhood dreams. Cord Dennison was rugged, handsome, and 100% *man*. His dark close-cropped hair set off widening crystal blue eyes, the color more intense than any of her faded memories. No wonder she'd been so smitten all those years.

Nanna leaned close and whispered in her ear, jerking her back to reality. "You might want to close your mouth before it gets stuck open."

2

*B*efore Cord stepped into the Buchanan's kitchen, he stopped to complete his phone conversation in private.

"But I don't want to take advantage of your generosity, Mr. Anderson."

"The way I see it, you've stayed right on target with this project, and it's only costing us half your salary."

Cord wasn't surprised at his boss' good-natured laugh. Finn Anderson, one of the four kingpins at Phantom Enterprises, had proven his compassion as often as his intellect. Cord had been working sixteen hours a day trying to juggle all his responsibilities and keep everyone happy. If only he wasn't fighting a growing desire to stay in Sage Valley, all would be good.

"I really appreciate you letting me work online." Cord hesitated. Anderson deserved nothing short of complete honesty. "But I need to tell you something else. Since I've been back, I feel like… like maybe I belong here, instead of New York."

The blood pulsed like a base drum in Cord's ears as the seconds ticked by.

"Cord, you have to do what's best for you, but I won't give up easy. I recruited you away from Abrams-Madison because I thought your background in creative software development made you perfect for this job. And I was right. As usual." He chuckled. "Let's keep this dialogue open. When you call each week, you can tell me what you're thinking."

"Thanks, Mr. Anderson."

"Finn," he corrected.

Though his larger-than-life boss was only five years older, Cord had a hard time calling him by his first name. Almost too nice to be real, Finn was likely a genius as far as Cord could tell. Yet he'd confessed that he didn't intend to have a family or even marry, which seemed odd to Cord. If the talk around the water-cooler was correct, there were plenty of women who'd volunteer to change Finn's mind, if they got the chance.

"Thank you, Finn. I'll call you next week and give you an update."

As was the custom, Cord didn't knock before stepping inside the Buchanans' back kitchen entrance. Sharon had an open-door policy after eight o'clock. Per her request, he'd been dropping by each morning to let her know how things were progressing. That she always offered some delicious treat made him more than happy to give a daily report. His mouth was already watering.

"Good morning, Sharon. I ran into Peter down at the stable…" His words died on his lips as his eyes adjusted to the interior light, focusing on a woman. Definitely not Mrs. Buchanan. Much younger. And absolutely breathtaking. Dark lashes defined mysterious almond eyes, the color of gray smoke. At a glance, the rest of her face was just as stunning, with a pert nose and lush lips, her jaw more determined than delicate. But those eyes… they were mesmerizing. He could stare into their beguiling depths for the rest of his life.

"Morning, Cord," Sharon said, bustling at the kitchen counter. "Would you like some hot chocolate? I was trying to convince Jessica she needs to eat more than a protein bar for breakfast."

The gray eyes blinked, breaking the spell. "Uhmm… I guess I could stay and eat a little something."

Jessica. Sharon spoke the intriguing stranger's name as if they'd already met. She must've gone to Sage Valley High, though he couldn't place her. He'd better play it cool —pretend he knew who she was.

"I'd love some hot chocolate," he replied, removing his hat. "But I can come back later, if you were in the middle of something."

"No worries. You can stay." A shy smile broke on Jessica's lips.

"Would you like a homemade biscuit with some cactus jelly?" asked Sharon.

"Yes, ma'am. I'd love it." He hung his hat on a wall hook and slid into a chair at the rustic round table, casting a surreptitious glance toward Jessica. He had to say something, to act like he remembered her. Maybe he'd get a clue about her identity. "What are you up to these days, Jessica?"

A perfect eyebrow arched, as if she could see through his ploy. "Working here for the summer. Then back to UNT Dallas for my last year."

Some quick math told him she was four to six years younger than his twenty-seven. Maybe that's why he didn't recognize her. He relaxed, feeling the expectations were lowered.

"You didn't tell me you hired someone new, Sharon. I'll need to figure it in to the expenses." He kept a smile on his face, though he worried Sharon and Peter were hiring more summer help without consulting him. The pair seemed to have on blinders about the financial state of the ranch.

"Don't worry," Sharon said, with a cheerful wink. "This employee is worth her weight in gold."

At his appraising glance, the girl lifted her chin. Hopefully, Sharon was right about Jessica. Her jeans and well-worn western boots were a good sign.

"What will you do when you graduate?" he asked, thinking a local girl might major in something related to agriculture.

"I'll have a degree in Math, with a certificate to teach high school." She took a chair across the table, sliding a full mug of steaming cocoa in front of him.

"Math, huh? I have to say, I didn't care much for calculus." He took a sip of cocoa.

"That's okay," Jessica replied. "I don't think accountants have much use for calculus."

He choked on his drink, his eyes watering. *How does she know I'm an accountant? Who is she?*

"Are you okay?" Jessica asked.

Was that a smirk on her lips? Did she realize he was only pretending to know who she was?

"I'm fine," he rasped. "It was a little hotter than I expected."

Sharon set a plate of biscuits in front of him. He took advantage of the distraction to stall for time, slathering a biscuit with butter and jelly while considering the mystery.

He felt her gaze on the top of his bent head. Desperate to divert her attention, he pointed to her untouched mug. "Aren't you going to eat a biscuit?"

She selected a biscuit and sliced it open to add butter and jelly. "Whatever happened to Picasso?"

He froze with his biscuit in front of his open mouth. "You knew my horse?"

"I met her a few times when you rode her to our house." She smiled and blinked her long lashes.

I have to recognize this girl. I've been to her house.

"Actually, Picasso is gone. I have a mare named Blaze."

"But you remember riding to my house, right?" Wide gray eyes blinked at him.

"Uhmm…"

Sharon joined them at the table. "Jess, stop torturing him. Tell him who you are."

Jess burst into laughter behind her hand. "I can't, Nanna. It's too fun."

"Nanna?" he repeated, his mind racing. She must be

one of Nick's cousins. Wait… Nick's baby sister? "Are you J.J.?"

"Jessica Jolene, at your service." Her cheeks flushed, which only served to make her prettier, if that was possible, the blush emphasizing an adorable smattering of freckles. "My friends call me Jess. No one calls me J.J. except Nick."

"I talked to Nick two weeks ago. He didn't tell me you were working here this summer." Cord was already rehearsing a tongue-lashing for the next time he spoke to his best friend.

"Nick didn't know until yesterday. I can't tell him anything without him throwing a fit, like I'm a little girl instead of a grown woman." Jessica leaned back and crossed her arms, her full lips forming an oh-so-kissable pout.

What am I doing? I can't think about kissing Nick's sister. He'd skin me alive.

Cord didn't mention that up until a few seconds ago, he'd thought of her as a thirteen-year-old kid. "Your brother can be a little overprotective."

"A little? Are you kidding me? He's offered to beat up every guy I ever dated."

Cord nodded. "That sounds like Nick."

"I think it comes from all those bull-riding competitions he used to do. He's got way too much testosterone." Even though she was complaining, she sounded proud of her big brother, who'd never managed to talk Cord into trying the dangerous sport. Hearing the admiration in her voice made him wish he had.

"I can't believe I didn't recognize you," he said.

"I probably still had braces when you graduated."

Her even white smile attested to the success of her orthodontics, but he couldn't remember her teeth being crooked. In truth, he'd probably ignored her altogether when she was nothing but Nick's pesky baby sister. Back then, Nick had been obsessed with Katie Crowley, the homecoming queen, while Cord had been preoccupied with competing for Valedictorian. Nine years later, Cord still concentrated on his work, finding that most women demanded too much attention.

"You've been gone from Sage Valley for nine years," Sharon said. "A lot has changed, including Jess. I'm not surprised you didn't recognize her."

Without thinking, his eyes dropped to check out her form, admiring the ways she'd certainly changed, until his gaze rose to meet her furious one. Hot liquid rushed into his face, and he gave himself a mental slap.

Attempting to cover his rude ogling, he said, "I noticed your boots. Can you ride a horse?"

Her jaw jutted forward. "Better than you."

"That sounds like a challenge," he said, desperate for a way to impress her. He might be a bit rusty, but he was fast, especially riding Blaze. "We should race."

"Bad idea." Sharon shook her head at Cord. "Jess is the Southwest Regional Barrel Racing Champion."

"I *was* the champion," she corrected. "I haven't raced in two years, Nanna."

So much for that idea. She obviously rode faster than he ever could.

Sharon came to his rescue. "Why don't you tell Jess about your plans for the ranch rodeo?"

His chest swelled. The rodeo was his pet project—one that was sure to benefit the ranch in a major way. "T-Bar-X had to drop out of the ranch rodeo circuit this summer, and I snagged their spot for Sage Valley."

Jessica's gray eyes grew round as saucers. "An amateur rodeo? Here? That's fantastic!"

"Back in the day, we held a rodeo here every summer," said Nanna. "So we already have the arena."

"Of course, we need to build or rent some more bleachers for an event this big," Cord added. "But that won't be a problem, since every single guest house is already rented at double the normal rates," he said, proudly. "Our staff will work the event, and we get a percentage of the ticket price as well."

"Is Mason McCaffrey entered in bull-riding?" Grinning, Jess sat forward, rubbing her hands together.

Cord wanted her to be enthused, but not about Mason McCaffrey. The man was a thorn in Cord's side. He'd been employed as the Sage Valley Ranch manager for the past four years. But he'd grown lazy, neglecting his duties while he gave his attention to rodeo competitions. Mason argued that he needed to maintain his reputation as a bull rider to attract visitors. However, Sage Valley was more than a dude ranch—it was a working cattle ranch. When Cord confronted Mason about mismanaging the cattle, the stubborn cowboy blew him off. Even though a records audit showed a steady decline in livestock profits, with income from the dude ranch holding the business afloat, until a decline in reservations the past two years.

"I'm sure he'll compete," Cord answered Jess, holding back the criticism on the tip of his tongue.

"He's still number one in the amateur bull-riding circuit, right?" she asked.

Cord frowned at her rapt expression. He'd never understood the term "starry-eyed" before. If only he could tell her how Mason's inattentiveness had almost cost her grandparents their ranch.

"I'm not sure how he's ranked," he said. "Do you know him?"

She nodded, her eyes darting to study her fingernails. "We went out a few years back. Nothing serious. After Nick finished competing, I always rooted for Mason. I love to watch bull riding."

Cord's stomach tied itself into a thousand knots as he imagined Jess, sitting in the stands at the Sage Valley Ranch Rodeo, cheering while Mason rode a madly bucking bull, swooning as he leapt to safety after eight seconds and waved his hat in the air. The image played as clearly as a digital video recording in his mind. And something in Cord's head snapped, all common sense vanishing in an instant. From his mouth leapt seven words that left him as shocked as his slack-jawed companions.

"I'm doing the bull riding competition, too."

ord held the phone away from his ear as Nick yelled, "Have you lost your mind? You can't compete in bull riding. You've never done it before."

"That's not true," Cord defended. "I rode once down at *Gilley's.*"

"That wasn't a bull." Nick continued to shout. "That was a mechanical box in a dancehall. And if I remember correctly, it bucked you off in two seconds onto a padded floor, and you could barely walk afterwards."

Forty-eight hours after Cord's hasty declaration, he'd only managed to dig himself into a deeper hole. In the wake of Jessica's excitement, he'd blathered some nonsense about taking up bull riding during a summer internship in Houston, which was sort of true, if you counted the mechanical bull. Then Mason McCaffrey, who'd previously refused to listen to his advice, declared that anyone with the guts to ride a rodeo bull must not be a stuck-up, citified, worthless, bag of air after all. The two actually had a long and productive discussion about how to trim the fat, so to speak, on the cattle production.

"Please, Nick. I've got six weeks to train. I don't have to win. I just need to not make a fool of myself. Can't you teach me?"

"No. And I can't believe you called me at the crack of dawn to ask this question. Did you think I'd answer in my sleep and agree?"

"I thought you were my best friend who would help me in my time of need."

"I'm not going to help my *best friend* commit suicide."

"You rode a bunch of times without dying." Cord presented the argument he'd been using to bolster his courage.

"It's not the same at all, you idiot. I started on easier bulls and worked my way up to rodeo bulls. I had hours and hours of practice."

"That's why I need to practice a few times before the real rodeo. You have to help me."

"Back out of the competition," Nick said. "Forfeit your entry fee, if you have to."

"I can't."

"Why not?" he demanded.

"It's a matter of pride." Cord gave Nick an explanation that didn't involve his sister. "I already told Mason McCaffrey I'm competing."

"McCaffrey's the best amateur bull rider around there. You're never going to beat him."

"I only need to stay on that bull long enough to earn Mason's respect. I'm finally making progress with him."

After a moment of silence, Nick let out a heavy sigh. "Four seconds would probably do it."

Cord let out a whoop of triumph. "So you'll teach me?"

"I'm in the middle of my summer semester at dental school. I barely have time to eat and sleep, much less drive from Houston to Sage Valley to give you bull riding lessons."

His premature celebration plummeted. "I guess I'm going to die, then."

"You're not going to die. But you're going to hurt. A lot."

"What do you mean?"

"I've got a buddy who gives bull riding lessons in Houston. They do group lessons, mostly to city dudes with more macho than common sense, which fits you to a T. It's Friday to Sunday, and it's not cheap. But he can at least teach you how to look like a bull rider during the two seconds before you get bucked off."

"You said I needed to stay on *four* seconds to earn Mason's respect."

"Yeah, but four seconds would take a miracle." Nick's laughter rang in his ear. "I gotta come watch this. Never thought I'd see the day."

"Thanks a lot," he sugared his words with sarcasm.

"I'm sorry, man." Nick caught his breath. "Honestly, if you're going to do this, the main thing you need to practice is jumping up from the ground into a full-blown sprint. That's how you stay alive."

Cord clung to the vain hope that he wouldn't embarrass himself. He couldn't stand the thought of Jessica laughing at him. Which reminded him that Nick had let him down in that regard.

"By the way, why didn't you tell me when you found out your sister was working here this summer?"

"Why should you care that J.J.'s staying with Nanna and Bucky?" Too perceptive for his own, good, Nick sounded suspicious.

"No reason." Cord used an indifferent tone.

"Should I report where Zander and Cohen are going on their vacations?"

"I don't care where your brothers go on vacations, but your sister is here. And like an idiot, I didn't recognize her."

"Ha! That's hilarious. I guess you haven't seen her in a while. That's what you get for running off to New York and never coming back."

"I think you set me up on purpose," Cord accused.

"Sad to say, I didn't do that. Although I would've if I'd thought of it."

"With friends like you…"

"Who needs any other friends? I know, right?"

"Funny, Nick."

"I have a great idea," Nick said, with enthusiasm.

"I doubt I'm going to agree."

Undaunted, Nick continued, "You'll be my watch dog. I don't want Jess dating anyone in Sage Valley, so you can be in charge of keeping all the guys away from her."

I guess now's not the time to tell Nick I'm interested in Jess.

"Why don't you want her dating?"

"Her fiancé just broke up with her, and she's primed for a rebound relationship."

Cord's fingers balled into fists, knowing someone had hurt her.

And what kind of jerk would I be to take advantage of her when she's vulnerable?

"When did it happen?" Cord asked.

"Back in January."

"It's been four months. She might be over it, right?"

"Believe me, her judgment's impaired. She's too emotional."

"She could meet a nice guy here. Don't you want her to be happy?"

"I don't want her to end up with a local guy." Nick's words sounded like they squeezed through tight lips. "I didn't much like her fiancé, but at least he was a ticket out of Sage Valley. I sure don't want her dating Mason McCaffrey this summer. She used to be all moony for him, just because he won some bull riding competitions."

"Funny criticism, coming from another bull rider."

"The dude's way too old for her," Nick's volume kicked up a notch. "He graduated the same year as us."

"Five years older isn't so bad," Cord said, defending himself more than Mason.

"If she starts dating McCaffrey, the next thing you know she'll be married and living in a rundown farmhouse with four kids hanging on her legs. She deserves a sophisticated city life. Speaking of city life, when are you going back to New York? Aren't you worried you're going to lose your job with Phantom Enterprises?"

"No, my new bosses are amazing. When they heard Dad had terminal cancer, they told me to take all the time I need. I took a temporary pay cut to keep working online through the summer while I get my folks' house fixed up to sell. But it's hard to find a decent contractor."

"When you sell the ranch, you won't have any reason to ever go back to Sage Valley," Nick said.

Cord couldn't bring himself to share his decision to stay in Sage Valley permanently. His friend would claim he'd gone insane. And Cord wouldn't blame him.

Determined to have a more exciting life, Cord left for college in New York City, vowing never to return. And he'd kept that promise for nine years, even enticing his family to come to New York for the holidays. But something happened during those last weeks with his family before his father died of cancer, something too complicated to explain, even to his best friend.

"I'll keep an eye on J.J. for you," Cord said.

"Do a little digging. If Mason or any other guy tries to make a move on my sister, tell him he'll have to answer to me."

Awesome. If the bull doesn't kill me, Nick will.

"Good morning, Shadow." The early morning sun

filtered through the cracks in the stable walls, painting distorted stripes across her horse's gray face. Jessica entered the stall with a bucket of oats and rubbed his side, twisting away when the gelding nosed her back jeans pocket. "Yes, I've got a carrot for you, but it's for later. I'll be back in a minute, after you eat your oats."

Shadow snorted, ignoring the oats Jess poured into his grain trough.

"I need to feed the others."

He answered with a heavy breath through his flared nostrils, lowering his head toward her. She obediently stroked the white patch on his forehead.

"There's no need to be jealous, you know. I don't like those other horses. And I've sworn off all guys until further notice. All guys… even Cord Dennison." Her throat tightened. "I admit, he's cute, and the fact that he's taking a pay cut to help my grandparents is pretty awesome. But I made a decision, and I'm sticking to it. I'm not dating until after graduation. I don't trust myself. What if it's nothing but physical attraction again? You can't build a relationship based on that. It won't last."

He shook his head and let out a nicker.

"What? You don't believe me? I promise, it's true. Absolutely no guys in my life until after college."

Shadow's head turned, and he eyed her sideways.

"Oh! Except for my brothers and you, of course."

She patted his shoulder, and he reached around to nuzzle her pocket again. Backing away, she laughed.

"Okay, you can have it." She retrieved the carrot, holding it out with flat fingers, and Shadow snatched it with his lips, crunching away with a rather triumphant expression.

"Shadow, you make me look like I don't have any willpower. But I do. I'm strong. Unbendable. Resolute."

Still chewing he pushed his nose against her neck, and she rubbed his muzzle.

With a few more pats on his side, she picked up her bucket, backed out of the stall and locked the gate. A deep "Howdy," sounded behind her, and she jumped, a squeal escaping her lips. Swirling around, she swatted at the offender, who happened to be Cord.

"Good gravy! You scared me to death."

He flinched but sported an unrepentant grin. "Sorry."

Her hand covered her racing heart, an anomaly related more to his magnetic presence than the sudden surprise. How long had he been standing there? Had he heard her conversation with Shadow? She mustered her sternest frown, the effect most likely diminished by the stray hair that fell across her face. As she blew it out of the way, she scolded him. "You shouldn't sneak up on people like that. What are you doing here, anyway?"

"I was looking for Gabe."

"He's probably still snoozing in his bunk. When I volunteered for the early morning shift for the summer, Gabe and Holden agreed, before I could change my mind." She carried her empty bucket to the oat bin, trying to avoid direct contact with those deadly eyes. His heavy boot steps told her he was right behind her.

"But aren't you leading both trail rides and the guest informational sessions? That's a lot of work."

"I've got to earn my keep." She dared a glance at him. *Big mistake.* He sported a blue t-shirt that not only brought out the sapphire of his eyes, but also emphasized his broad shoulders. Her heart kicked into a higher gear.

He leaned his shoulder against the wall. "I'm surprised you're up so early, since you're a city girl now."

"A man who spent the last nine years in New York shouldn't be criticizing me about living in the city." She shot a glance over her shoulder, in time to see him wince, and regretted her hasty retort.

"A big city has a lot to offer," he mumbled.

She shouldn't make him feel bad about wanting to escape their small country town. She'd felt the same way until a few months ago.

"I've enjoyed Dallas since I transferred to UNT from Tarleton." She forced a positive note in her voice. "There's always something exciting going on." She left off the part where dating Parker Brown had made her long to be back home with plain old country folks. After all, just because Parker's family and friends were snobby socialites didn't mean there weren't nice people living in cities. To be honest, she liked everyone well enough until Parker gave her the boot and skinned her pride.

"I guess you're glad you aren't still living in Sage Valley, like some of our friends from high school."

His comment gave her a sense of déjà vu. Where had she heard that before? *Nick!* Her sneaky big brother was using Cord to get to her. To convince her she belonged in the city.

Well, it isn't going to work. Nick needs to mind his own business.

"I'm glad I went off to college, but I don't have anything against Sage Valley." She stuck a defiant chin in the air, daring Cord to contradict her. "And you can tell Nick to butt out of my life."

His guilty grimace confirmed her suspicions. "He's just worried about you."

"He treats me like I'm ten, instead of twenty-two. He can't control where I live or who I date."

"I agree. I'll tell him so." Cord accented his words with sharp nod. "I'll say, 'Stay out of Jessica's life. Whether you like it or not, she's dating…' Who did you say you were dating?"

Jess rotated her gaze up to the heavens. "Nice try. But I'm not telling."

"You wouldn't be interested in a guy like McCaffrey, would you? I mean, don't you want to date someone who's been to college, like you?"

She ought to tell him she wasn't dating anyone until she graduated. It would put him out of his misery. *But where's the fun in that?*

Her theater teacher would've been proud of her reaction. She lifted her shoulders high and let them fall, twisting her mouth to the side, as if she were contemplating the pros and cons of dating McCaffrey. "You don't have to go to college to be smart. And Mason has other assets, if you know what I mean." She gave Cord a sassy wink, designed to make smoke come out of his ears, and she was pretty sure she succeeded.

"He may be the top bull rider around here," Cord said, with a sullen expression. "But you can never trust a guy like that. Bull riders have girls hanging all over them."

"Is that why you signed up for the bull riding event?"

Even with the speckled sunlight mottling his face, she saw red race up his neck to the tips of his ears.

"No," he muttered.

Grinning, she turned to refill her bucket. When she reached onto the shelf for the grain scoop, a yowl rent the air, gray fur flashing past her face. She stumbled backwards as Titus, the ever-grumpy barn cat, sailed by, smacking her with his tail. The bucket slipped from her fingers and landed with a clang, as she staggered against Cord's rock-hard chest, his strong grasp steadying her, his chuckle rumbling against her back.

Her hot face was probably redder than Cord's.

"Kind of jumpy today, aren't you?" His voice was tinged with humor.

She shook herself free from his tempting arms. "Anyone with common sense gets out of the way when Titus is coming through. That cat is a menace."

"Yes, I met him my first day." Cord tipped the brim of his hat back, squinting at her head. "Hold still. Titus knocked something into your hair."

She held her breath as his hand stretched toward her forehead. Gentle fingers touched her hair, and chill bumps rifled down her neck and spine. His hand withdrew, grasping an inch-long piece of string.

"Thanks." She struggled to swallow.

His eyes, brilliant pieces of sky, trapped hers in a para-lyzing gaze.

"I feel sorry for Titus," he said, still holding her captive with his soul-piercing blue orbs as his fingers held the tattered string that looked about as strong as her willpower.

"You do?" she breathed.

His lids closed halfway. "He's just cranky because he's lonely. He's been isolated way too long."

She jerked her gaze away from his hypnotic trance. "It's his own fault he's alone. Have you ever tried to pet Titus?"

"I made that mistake the first time we crossed paths. I admit, he drew blood. But I'm determined to make friends with him. By the end of the summer, he'll be eating out of my hand."

"More like he'll be *eating* your hand."

"We'll see."

A delectable dimple winked into view, which made him look even more attractive, a fact that irritated her like a bur under a saddle. She couldn't let herself fall for Cord, especially when his only interest was in spying on her brother's behalf.

Though she was closest in age to Nick and confided in him more than her other two brothers, he tended to be as meddling as Nanna. In his younger years, Nick had often teased that the family found her in a basket on the side of the road, his explanation for her appearance, markedly different from her brothers. All three of them were over six feet tall, with the same sandy brown hair, while she was shorter, at five four, her hair dark brown.

This was one of those times she wished she had a sister to confide in. Cord was so tempting, but her failed relationship with Parker had shaken her more than she admitted to her grandmother. It was as if he'd stripped her self-confidence away. She was determined not to let that happen again. No dating until graduation. On the other hand, she would make it her goal to keep Cord and Nick fretting about her love life all summer.

That's what they get for interfering.

---

4

*C*ord stole another glance at the stairwell as he swallowed the last of his coffee. His third cup. If Jess didn't hurry down, he was going to float away. Over the past two weeks, the morning stops at the Buchanans' kitchen had become his favorite part of the day. Not simply because Sharon was an excellent cook, but because it was almost his only chance to see Jessica. Her daily schedule was as hectic as his, especially now, since one of their most competent volunteer staffers had sprained his ankle. That left Cord filling in on the canoe and kayak trips.

The morning encounters in the company of her grandmother, and sometimes her grandfather, as well, were as close as he came to a private encounter with Jess, and he loved every minute. From her easy laugh to her quick temper and feisty comebacks, she proved even more intriguing than his initial impressions. Extremely careful to hide his feelings, he was sure no one suspected his increasing interest.

Since he took his noon meal in the restaurant with the guests, his only other chance to spend time with Jess was during dinner, surrounded by all the other employees. After the evening meal, he left for his family's ranch, leaving Jessica alone with the flirtatious ranch hands and male guest staffers. Not that he would've tried to intervene. He had no doubt she'd rake him over the coals if he did. After a careful analysis, he determined his only chance with Jessica was to somehow make himself more appealing than his competition.

He eyed his empty coffee cup. Should he ask for a fourth?

"If you're looking for Jess, she's already gone out for the morning," said Sharon, with a knowing smile. "Something about needing to adjust one of the bridles before the trail ride."

"Oh, I wasn't waiting for her or anything." He cleared his throat, buying time while coming up with an excuse. "You know… I have those latest forecast figures. They're based on auction rates from the last six months. Bucky might want to see them."

"Yeah, right." Sharon's raised eyebrows told him his interest in Jess wasn't as secret as he'd thought. She pushed up from the table, elbowing Bucky, whose face was hidden behind the newspaper.

"What?" He lowered the paper, lifting his chin to peer at his wife through his bifocals.

"Let Cord show you those numbers so he can get out of here." She rinsed her dishes in the sink.

"He said he wasn't in a hurry."

"He is now."

"I am?" Cord frowned. Trying to keep up with Sharon's train of thought was always a challenge. Today was no exception.

Patting her hands dry with a dish towel, she tossed it on the counter. "You are if you want to catch Jessica before she leaves on the morning trail ride."

"Why would I need to do that?"

She put her hands on her hips and tilted her head, studying him like she could read his mind, but it was in a foreign language. "Didn't you send out an email last night, announcing that you moved the annual dance up to the Friday night of the rodeo weekend?"

"Yes. And today, I should get confirmation on the cover band."

"Do you know who Jess eats lunch with almost every single day after the morning trail ride?"

He didn't know, but he could guess. "Mason McCaffrey?"

His stomach twisted even before she nodded affirmation.

"Her big brother wouldn't want her to go to the dance with Mason, would he? Didn't you tell me you were guarding her for Nick?"

With great difficulty, he stopped his jaw from dropping open. How did she know this stuff? "I'm pretty sure I didn't tell you that."

"You didn't?" Sharon frowned, tapping a finger on her cheek. Then her eyebrows shot up, and she pointed the finger toward him. "That's right. Jess told me. Mad as a hornet about it, too." She flapped a loose hand at Cord. "Doesn't matter how I found out. The point is, Mason's probably going to invite her to that dance if you don't beat him to it."

He picked up his coffee cup in trembling fingers and held it to his mouth, hoping Sharon wouldn't notice it was empty. "Nick doesn't want *any* guy from Sage River dating his sister. That includes me."

Bucky waved for attention. "I don't understand. What does all this have to do with the auction figures?"

"Nothing, dear." Sharon leaned down with her hands on his shoulders and kissed him on his bald spot. "Go back to your paper."

Cord saw Bucky's eyes roll before the newspaper covered them again.

With her hand on Cord's elbow, Sharon guided him up from the table toward the door. She spoke in a lowered voice. "It doesn't matter what Nick thinks. Jess has a mind of her own."

"Don't you think Jessica would be mad if she knew you were interfering? She sure got upset when I tried it."

Sharon heaved a heavy sigh. "I know I shouldn't meddle. My children have fussed at me for years, but it's such a hard habit to break." Her hand gripped Cord's arm. "I want you to ignore everything I said. Pretend you didn't hear a word."

"Yes, ma'am. I'll try," he said, doubtfully.

"And don't tell Jessica I said anything."

"I won't."

"And forget that stuff I told you about Mason's arrest record."

"Arrest record?"

"I didn't tell you? Good. It'll be easier to forget. He's a good kid, or Bucky wouldn't have hired him." Her hand covered her eyes, thumb and fingers rubbing her temples. "Doesn't mean I want him married to my granddaughter, though."

"Married? Don't you think you're jumping the gun a little bit? They aren't even dating." The blood pounded in Cord's ears. "At least, I don't think they are."

Sharon's hand applied pressure to his back, shuffling him through the door. "I'm sure you're right, Cord. I'm just a doddering old lady. I know you'll do the right thing."

The door clicked shut, and he was standing outside, the sweat trickling down his back from something other than the oppressive Texas heat.

Cord was at his best when working with a plan, so he'd plotted a detailed course of action to win Jessica. He'd envisioned using their morning breakfasts to gradually get to know each other, culminating with the bull-riding competition to impress her with his bravery. But if Mason was actively pursuing Jess, Cord needed to step up his game. He couldn't afford to wait four more weeks until the rodeo.

Asking Jessica to the dance wasn't a bad idea, but she was bound to be suspicious of his motives. Every time he thought he was making progress with her, she accused him of spying for Nick. Eventually, Cord intended to tell her the truth… that his desire to spend time with her had nothing whatsoever to do with following her brother's orders, and everything to do with the fact that he liked her.

Maybe now's the time.

His stomach rolled in a series of somersaults.

Or not.

"I'M BUSY RIGHT NOW, MASON." Focused on Shadow as she led him out of the stall, Jessica didn't hear what Mason was saying. He'd been hanging around more often, all too encouraged by the attention she'd thrown his direction. What a mistake! Her efforts to worry her buttinsky brother had backfired in a big way. And all for nothing. Cord hadn't even been around to see her flirting with Mason. "Can we talk after the trail ride?"

Mason fell in step beside her, his ever-present cowboy hat shading his eyes as they stepped outside. From the piece of straw clinging to his tank top, she assumed he'd been putting out hay this morning. She noted two female guests, the only coeds in today's trail ride group, gawking at his exposed muscles. Ordinarily, he would've preened under their attention. Today, however, he was focused on Jess. "Sure, I'll save you a seat at lunch."

She turned her mind to the task at hand, tucking the brim down on the open-weave straw cowboy hat she wore to protect against the sun. The cloudless sky promised sweltering heat by the time the ride was over, at noon. Thankfully, the majority of the trail wandered under the trees, along the river.

"See ya later." She tried to dismiss Mason, but he caught her elbow.

"Wait. You didn't answer my question."

Ughh! He'd probably asked her on another date. So far, she'd managed to find excuses to avoid going out with him. The guy was as tenacious as a coonhound on a scent trail. Confessing she didn't intend to date anyone until after graduation would only increase his efforts to wear her down. The one sure dissuasion would be swearing she wasn't interested in him, a conversation which was bound to hurt his feelings.

"Can't we do this at lunch?" she suggested, still moving toward the line of trail horses and waiting guests.

"But I wanted to make sure I was the first to ask you." He tilted his head, looking out from under the brim of his hat.

"Ask me what?"

"To go to the dance with me. Didn't you see the email this morning? The annual dance got moved up to rodeo weekend."

She stopped in her tracks as her mind scrambled for a new alibi. He'd already asked her to be his date for the annual dance at the end of summer. The fact that her college classes started in mid-August had provided a perfect excuse. *Now what can I say?*

Shadow snorted his impatience at the delay. She'd put it off as long as she could. She had to be honest with Mason, but she hated to embarrass him while a bunch of guests milled around within earshot.

"Mason… I… uhmm… I'm…"

Giggles from the two female guests distracted her, and she followed their slack-jawed stares. Cord was striding toward the trail ride gathering… all six feet of him, with lean rippling muscles and a face that could've been in movies. No wonder the women were salivating over the guy.

"I'm in love with that cowboy," the brunette girl gushed, with a husky chuckle.

"He's mine." The blonde flipped her long braid to her back, exposing her shoulder, naked except for the tiny spaghetti strap on her barely-there top. "He sat by me at lunch, yesterday."

Jessica fought an insane urge to chop off the thick plait of hair and toss it into the nearby horse trough.

What's wrong with me?

"Jess?" Mason tapped her arm, his earnest expression reminding her of his pending invitation.

In the desperation of the moment, Jessica blurted out, "I'm going to the dance with Cord."

CORD SPIED Jessica beside the guests lined up for the trail ride. He was hurrying to catch her before she started her instructions when he noticed who was with her.

Mason McCaffrey. I may be too late.

Funny that before Sharon mentioned asking Jessica to the dance, it hadn't even crossed his mind. Now, the thought of her swinging to the music in anyone's arms but his had him seeing red. But was he ready to swallow his pride and admit he liked her? Right here and now, in front of Mason and all these Sage Valley guests?

He was so intent on reaching her that he forgot to watch where he was stepping. Almost there, the sound of his footstep changed from a clunk on hard-packed dirt to a sloppy squish, and he realized his mistake. The horses had left fresh piles of dung, and like a city slicker, he'd stepped right in one.

Maybe no one saw me.

He heard a partially stifled snicker, and looked over to see two familiar coeds laughing at his expense.

No such luck.

He tipped his hat in awkward acknowledgment, knowing the guests were delighted to see the staff make such an embarrassing misstep. Rubbing his caked sole on the hard ground, he made a vain attempt to wipe the fresh manure from his boot. With any luck, Jess, who was busy tying Shadow's reins to a post, would never even notice.

"Nice job, Dennison." Mason's lip curled in a rather nasty sneer, as if Cord had thrown the excrement at him instead of stepping in it. "It's not too late to dump him, Jess. I can't believe you'd go to the dance with a greenhorn."

"Huh?" Cord frowned and rubbed the back of his neck, his gaze tracking from Mason's scowl to Jessica's wide eyes. "What are you talking about?"

"I'm saying you're as green as a drugstore cowboy," said Mason, his voice loud enough to draw attention from the guests.

"That's not what I meant." Cord disregarded the well-deserved insult. "You said something about the dance. About Jess and me——"

"It's okay, Cord." Jess cut him off in mid-sentence to grab his arm and propel him five feet away. She mumbled, "Please help me. Just roll with whatever I say."

"Uhmm…" Cord had no idea what was going on, but her pleading eyes had already melted his heart. He'd do anything to help her.

Jessica turned to face the glaring ranch manager. "Don't make a scene, Mason. Cord already asked me to the dance."

Cord hid his shock. Barely.

"This is bull, Jessica." Mason growled. "You and I… we had an understanding."

Cord wrapped his arm around Jessica's shoulder and pulled her against him. "I believe you had a *mis*-under-standing."

"When did the two of you start dating?" McCaffrey spat on the ground, eliciting a curled lip from Jessica.

She jerked her chin toward the curious onlookers. "Let's continue this conversation away from the guests."

With a glance at the line of involuntary eavesdroppers, McCaffrey huffed his begrudging agreement and clomped across the courtyard, stopping under a shady live oak tree. Cord and Jess followed after him.

When Mason swirled to face them, his tone seethed with suspicion. "You never mentioned him, Jess. I haven't ever seen you together. Not once."

"We were keeping it on the down-low," she said.

Despite her confident voice, Cord sensed her cringing at the lie. But the humor of the situation was beginning to set in. He couldn't resist taking advantage of her predicament.

"I guess there's no use hiding it, sweetheart." Cord slipped his arm around her waist and bent his head to kiss her cheek. His heart picked up speed as his lips slid down to her neck, lingering to breathe in her clean scent.

A stiff-as-plastic smile appeared on her face, and she murmured from the corner of her mouth. "I'm going to kill you."

He coughed, using a hand to hide his smile.

Mason, evidently, saw no humor in the situation. Hands clenched, the wiry cowboy lifted his chin. "I wouldn't try to steal another man's woman, Dennison. You should've told me she belonged to you."

"Hold on a minute." Jessica shook free from Cord's grasp and slammed her hands on her hips. "I don't *belong* to anyone."

Cord put a warning finger to his lips. "Shhh. Let me handle this."

She snapped her mouth closed, her lips pressed together in a tight white line, silent rage bulging behind her eyes.

"You're gonna have a tough time corralling that little filly." With a sour chuckle, McCaffrey slapped Cord's shoulder, then turned away. Bitterness tinged his voice. "Good luck."

Cord hated to alienate McCaffrey just when the stubborn ranch manager was finally beginning to listen to reason. Somehow, he had to do damage control without blowing Jessica's cover.

"Hey, Mason. Wait." Cord paused until the man turned back. "No hard feelings, right? I should've said something about Jess, but I was trying to keep her happy. You know how women can be."

Frozen in place, the muscles flexed along McCaffrey's jaw and his hands balled into fists. But rather than shouting a string of expletives, as Cord feared, Mason snorted with laughter.

"I don't know what you call it in the big city, but around here, we call that *hen-pecked*." Mason cackled as he sauntered away. "Don't forget to watch where you walk, greenhorn."

The moment Mason disappeared into the bunkhouse, slamming the door behind him, Jess twisted to confront Cord, her face stormy. His father had worn the same expression when, as a sixteen-year-old, Cord had wrecked his dad's brand new truck.

"You've done your good deed for the day." She bared her teeth as she squeezed the words out. "You can go, now."

Yikes! Digging himself out of this hole wasn't going to be easy.

"Why're you upset?" He tried to look innocent.

"Why am I upset?" Her hands flailed in the air. "Maybe because the two of you discussed me like a piece of property."

"That's just guy talk. I didn't mean it."

"Then you said that line, *you know how women are*."

When she quoted him, she lowered her voice and added a huge helping of whiny sarcasm.

She was so cute when she was mad, Cord had a crazy urge to egg her on. Instead, he found a morsel of common sense and forced himself to explain.

"I have to work with him every day. I need his cooperation."

"What about that kiss? You can't tell me you were trying to gain his cooperation with that."

"You said *roll with you*. I was *rolling*. Anyway, it was only a peck on the cheek."

"You kissed my neck," she squeaked, her face flaming. "In front of everybody."

Good thing he hadn't kissed her on the lips, like he'd wanted.

"I'm sorry." *I'm sorry it bothered you, but I'm not sorry it happened.*

"That's what I get for lying," she mumbled, her shoulders drooping like a popped balloon. "Humiliation."

"My kiss was humiliating?" Not exactly what he was aiming for.

"Stop teasing me." She snatched her straw hat off and gave him a playful swat on the arm. "I not only pretended you asked me to the dance, but I got caught lying about it. Pretty much the definition of mortification."

"If you didn't want to go with Mason, why didn't you just say no?"

"I don't know. He caught me by surprise, and I didn't want to hurt his feelings."

"Yeah. We men have such tender egos. You really have to be careful."

This time, he succeeded in coaxing a grin. "It's true. Men act tough on the outside, but inside they're like delicate china."

"Or eggshells," he suggested.

"Exactly." Her smiled widened, then faltered. "And it'll be eggshell powder when Mason finds out the truth."

He wanted to put that smile back on her face. More than anything.

"If we go to the dance together, he'll never find out."

Her eyebrows lifted. "Thanks for the offer, but we could never pull it off. It's not just the dance, anymore. We'd have to pretend to be dating for the next four weeks."

He drew his brows together, as if the idea were somewhat painful. "I'd be willing."

"Why would you do that?" she asked, crossing her arms and drumming her fingers. "Oh! I get it. Nick really doesn't want me dating Mason, does he?"

He couldn't let her believe that. She needed to know he had genuine feelings for her.

"You're right. Nick doesn't think Mason's good enough for you. But that's not—"

"Hey, Jess!" Holden called. "We're ready to go."

Startled, Cord twisted to look behind him. Holden had the entire group mounted and lined up on their horses.

"Cripes! I'm late." Jess started jogging toward them, and Cord hurried to stay with her. "I don't know, Cord. I'm still not sure we can make it believable."

"I think we can," he said, as they approached the head of the line, where Holden had Shadow waiting for her.

"We'll see," she mumbled, reaching for her horse.

But Cord caught her arm before she could grasp the reins and turned her toward him, drawing her against him. Her wide gray eyes stared up into his, and his heart threatened to crack his ribs open. Her mouth moved. She might've said something, but he couldn't hear it. The blood pounding in his ears drowned out everything in the universe.

"How's this for believable?" he muttered, lifting his hands to cradle her face. He lowered his mouth to hers, intending to place a short, firm kiss. But those lips! They were even more soft and sweet than he'd imagined. Once he had a taste, he wanted more. More of the plump responsive lips that made him forget every other kiss he'd ever had.

"Woo hoo! Ride 'em, cowboy."

Catcalls erupted, and Jess sprang back, blushing to the roots of her hair.

Without another word, she swung onto Shadow's back and kicked him forward.

"Only four seconds," said Holden as he ambled past and slapped Cord's shoulder. "Better luck next time, cowboy."

5

*J*essica managed to stay on her horse. That was about the sum total of her accomplishments on the trail ride following that bombshell kiss. The one that left her head spinning. When they reached the river, Holden rode up beside her and suggested he might enjoy taking the lead on this trip. Though he sported a wry grin, he avoided pointing out her absent state of mind. Still shell-shocked, she hadn't uttered a single word of her usual spiel, full of fun facts about Sage Valley Ranch. Grateful for his rescue, she followed at the end of the pack and let her mind process.

That kiss was forever seared into her memories. The instant their lips touched, her heart had stopped, along with her breathing. Then every nerve in her body fired at once, jumpstarting her still heart. In the matter of a few seconds, she'd died, gone to heaven, and come back to life.

Not that she was falling for him. She was simply reliving her seventh-grade crush. No doubt, Cord was attractive, but she wouldn't let herself get involved with another hunky guy who'd surely break her heart. That didn't mean she couldn't relish the feel of that kiss, and imagine it happening again.

"Don't forget to close the gate," Holden called back, shaking her out of her reverie.

How could she have daydreamed for the entire two-hour trail ride?

Dismounting to swing the gate closed, she side-stepped a fresh pile of manure, which reminded her of Cord's mishap. A smile crept onto her face. One of the things she found so charming was his athletic looks, in contrast to his general nerdiness. Not that he didn't know his way around a ranch, but he'd always been the studious type. Though he usually wore contacts, she actually preferred him with glasses, as if the dark frames were hiding his Superman persona.

Why had that kiss affected her so strongly when she knew it was only for show? She had to avoid him as much as possible. For the moment, he believed she'd only used him as an excuse to avoid going to the dance with Mason. But if she spent much time alone with Cord, she was liable to let something slip out. Imagine how humiliating it would be if he realized she actually liked him when his part was all an act.

Ughh! Awkward with a capital A.

Jess and Holden got all the guests safely dismounted and stabled the horses, a process that took another forty-five minutes, even with extra help from Gabe and a couple of the volunteer staff. Then Jess found a text message waiting on her cell phone from an unknown number.

Hi. This is Cord. Sorry about the kiss. Out of town for the weekend. We'll talk Monday.

Her mind churned, considering every possible meaning of his brief message. Was he sorry about the kiss because he regretted it? Where was he going for the weekend, leaving before noon on a Thursday? Frustrated and confused, she headed for a shower, with a detour by the ranch general store.

"Hi, Jess!" Lexi Turner greeted her when she walked in. "What do you need, today? More dark chocolate-covered almonds?"

"Actually, I need a new toothbrush. Do you have any?"

"Sure." She moved to the shelf with the hygiene supplies. "Did you wear your old one out?"

"No, I accidentally knocked it into the toilet."

Lexi let out a musical laugh. "Oh no! I hope there wasn't anything else in there."

"Thank goodness, I'd already flushed. But no amount of Clorox will make me use that toothbrush again."

"I agree. Glad we have a new one for you." Lexi grabbed three boxes off the shelf. "Red, blue, or green?"

"Surprise me." Jess held out her hand.

"You seem like a red person to me. Red personalities are active and cheerful and confident."

Jess stared at the brush in her hand. "That's the wrong color for me. I think I need the green, because I always get myself in a pickle."

"Don't be so hard on yourself. You're not the first

person to drop something in a toilet." Lexi lowered her voice as if someone could hear them, though no one else was in the shop. "Last month, I dropped my cell phone in."

"That's terrible, but this is worse. Way worse."

"Come on." Lexi moved to the deli counter, sliding onto a stool with cheery red and white polka dots. "Sit down and tell Dr. Lexi all about it."

"Can you keep a secret? I mean, you can't tell a soul. Especially not my Nanna."

"In my forty years on this earth, I've yet to reveal a secret. Even when staked to the ground and tortured for hours by someone singing *Baby Shark.*"

Jess couldn't help chuckling. "Now I know you're lying, because you can't possibly be forty years old."

With her flawless skin and a sassy short haircut, Lexi could've passed for someone in her twenties.

"We should trade bodies, then, because I swear you're the only twenty-two-year-old I know who's as mature as a forty-year-old."

Lexi patted the stool beside her, and Jessica sat down, only then realizing how tired she was.

Emotions are draining. I wish I could turn them off.

"I act older because I've worked my way through college. Makes you grow up fast when you're responsible for all those bills and loans." Jess propped her elbows on the counter, resting her chin on her hands.

"Your folks didn't help?" Lexi asked.

"The summer I finished high school, my dad's father had a stroke. Dad had to retire early and move up to Oklahoma to help him and work on the family farm. My folks helped as much as they could, but my three older brothers had already depleted the college fund."

"Pretty impressive for you to do it on your own."

Jess shrugged. "I did what I had to do. That's why I can't let myself date anyone until after I graduate. When I was with Parker, my grades dropped so low I almost lost my scholarship. I'm not going to make that mistake twice."

"Parker. He's that loser guy you were engaged to?"

"That's the one. But he wasn't really a loser as much as we weren't suited for each other."

"The guy didn't know a good thing when he had it. That makes him a loser in my book." Lexi cocked her head. "Is that what this is about? Are you feeling bummed because you miss your ex?"

"No way. But there's someone else…"

"You like someone?" Lexi's hands clapped together, delight on her face. "That's a good thing, right? Why are you so blue?"

All her pent-up feelings spewed out in an eruption of words. "I like him, but I know I shouldn't. And he only thinks of me as his friend's baby sister that he has to protect. So the kisses didn't mean anything. But everybody saw it, so they all think we're dating. So even though we're not dating, we need to break up. And if we break up, this other guy will ask me to the dance again, which is how this all started in the first place."

One skeptical eyebrow lifted, and Lexi blew out a long, slow breath. "I think I should make us some lunch. I have a feeling this is going to take a while."

Thirty minutes, one long story, and two sandwiches

later, Lexi dabbed her mouth with a napkin and swiveled her stool to lean against the counter.

"You're right. You need the pickle toothbrush."

"I know," Jess moaned. "It's a mess!"

"My gut feeling is you should tell Cord you like him. It might send him running. But who knows… maybe he'll realize you're more than Nick's kid sister. Believe me, five years of age difference is no big thing."

"No, no, no! You're supposed to help me *not* like him anymore. Then I don't have to worry about having another relationship mess up my last year of college. And I won't have to tell him anything."

"That's true," Lexi tapped a fingernail against her front tooth. "Plus, you said you don't think you could live in a big city."

"I guess I could, if I had to. But I've been living in Dallas for a while now, and all I can think of is how much I love Sage Valley."

Lexi stared at her water glass, as if the answer were written on the ice cubes. "Sure sounds like Cord's headed back to New York. He said Phantom Enterprises is his dream job."

"You were talking to Cord about his job?"

"I've been told I'm nosy." A grin danced onto her face. "He came by this morning to get some snacks for a weekend trip, so I grilled him."

"You see? That's a sign from God we're not supposed to be together."

"Maybe if he was with you, he'd change his mind."

"No, he'd be miserable, and it'd be my fault."

"But if you loved each other, you'd find a way around those things." Lexi took a long swallow of iced tea. "I guess the question is this. Do you like Cord? Or do you love him?"

"A few months ago, I thought I was in love with Parker. Then he broke the engagement. Now I don't know what I feel." Jess sighed. "It's obvious I can't trust my feelings."

"I don't know, Jess. The way you talk about Cord is different. To me, it sounds like you'd be really happy with him."

"I'll be happy, no matter what. I'm a Clark woman. My Nanna says we're survivors," said Jessica. "Cord's the one I'm worried about."

"Why?"

"Obviously, he's the kind of guy who'll sacrifice himself for someone else's happiness. He moved across the country and risked losing his dream job so he could be with his family when they needed him." Jess ticked off her points, finger by finger. "He's doing all this stuff to help my grandparents, even while he's working his other job online. He let my brother talk him into being my personal watch dog in addition to all his other responsibilities. He pretended we were dating, just to help me save face, even though he must've been embarrassed."

"You make some interesting arguments." Lexi stood up, stacking their dirty plates. "But I still think you should be honest with Cord and let him decide what's best for himself."

"What about my no-dating rule?"

"Rules are made to be broken. Take a chance... tell

him the truth." Lexi wiped off the counter. "Or I can tell him for you."

"Not unless you want to be tortured again."

"I kind of like *Baby Shark*, now." Lexi hummed the quirky tune as she carried the plates to the small sink.

"You promised me—"

"Just kidding. But he's gone 'til Monday. You might get your courage up by then."

"Where did he go?"

"He wouldn't say." Lexi moved to the register and rang up a ticket for the toothbrush. "He bought two boxes of protein bars and a bottle of ibuprofen. Then he joked that his will was under his mattress in case he didn't survive the weekend."

"I hope he wasn't serious." The hairs stood up on the back of Jessica's neck. "What could he be doing?"

"I don't know, but I'm literally dying to find out."

"I'M DYING." Cord groaned as he limped into the arena on the morning of day two. "Literally dying. Every inch of my body hurts. I must be bleeding internally."

Several of his classmates expressed similar opinions, but their instructor had zero sympathy.

"Three things in life are certain." Manual Lopez held three gloved fingers up, pacing in front of the group of young men as he spouted philosophy like a college profes-sor. Except this professor wore cowboy boots, chaps, and a single glove, as did each of his eight students. He continued his diatribe, counting off the so-called certainties. "Death. Taxes. And the fact that you *will* be thrown from *every* bull *every* single time you ride. Pain is part of the game, gentlemen. Get used to it."

"Tell me something I don't know," Cord muttered from his position, leaning against the wall, his bottom too sore to sit on the bench.

"Mr. Dennison…"

Cord cringed, attempting to shrink to invisibility. Why hadn't he kept his big mouth shut?

"Thank you for volunteering to go first today, Dennison," said Lopez, with a congenial smile. "We'll do one more round of warmups on Bully," he said, ambling over to the mechanical bull they'd been practicing on, a headless barrel with no resemblance to an animal. "Then it's on to Hurricane."

Right on cue, the live bull snorted in his stall across the arena, sending a shiver of apprehension down Cord's back. It hurt to fall off a mechanical bull, but at least he hadn't had to worry about being gored, kicked, or stepped on.

"What's the first rule of bull riding?"

Cord answered in unison with his classmates, "Never take your eyes off the bull."

"Very good. Cord, come on out here." Lopez patted Bully's back. "Once again, let's go over what to do when you get *hung up*."

Cord's mouth went drier than it had when he first saw Jessica. The idea of having his hand caught in the rope, to be dragged and stomped by a furious bull, was terrifying. After a day of lessons on a bucking barrel, Cord's respect for both Nick and Mason had doubled. Either that, or he'd decided the men were insane for pursuing the dangerous sport.

So what does that make me?

An idiot. All his fellow students were below the age of twenty-one, still young enough to feel immortal. Cord was old enough to know better, yet here he was, trying to prove his bravery at the ripe old age of twenty-seven.

Cord climbed on top of Bully and grasped the bull rope with his right hand. Then he rolled off to his left, a move which automatically twisted his hand under the rope.

"Good," Lopez nodded. "You know how to get hung up. But now what?"

"I stay close to the bull's shoulder and watch his head."

Another nod. "And that's easy to do when it's a motion-less Bully, instead of a 1500-pound twisting, bucking bull. What next?"

"I either jump up and throw my right elbow over the bull, or I find the rope tail with my left hand and push it over the top to untwist my hand."

Justin, one of the more outspoken students, said, "Or wait for the bullfighter to grab the rope tail for you."

Cord knew the bullfighters would risk their lives to save a bull rider. Without the seemingly fearless bullfighting crew, the riders might not make it to safety.

"The bullfighters will rescue you if you're hung up." Lopez gave Justin a measured look. "*Eventually.* Of course, you might get trampled by then."

This elicited a round of snickers.

"Not me," said Justin, with a laugh, pointing at Cord. "I was talking about Grandpa."

"Very funny," said Cord, who'd accepted constant teasing from the younger guys. "Just for that, I'll let you borrow my razor… when your beard comes in."

"Ooooo! Burn!" Lighthearted laughter rippled through the group.

"Back to business," Lopez cut in. "I want everyone to practice these techniques with Bully bucking and turning. Then we start the rounds with Hurricane. Rotate through as many times as you like. If anyone makes it to eight seconds, dinner's on me."

The boys whooped their excitement at facing their first real bull. All except Cord.

Lopez leaned close, lowering his voice. "Listen, Cord. If you don't want to ride Hurricane, I totally understand. Like I said before, your height's going to make it harder to balance. Six feet is pretty tall for a bull rider."

"That rider from Australia is six foot two," Cord said, stubbornly. "I'll fall, just like the short guys. Then I'll run. I was a sprinter in high school."

"A long time ago," Lopez reminded him.

"I'm not quitting."

Lopez stared at him, his gaze so intense Cord couldn't look away. He must've finally seen what he was looking for because his mouth twisted in a crooked smile. He put his hat back on, then slapped the side of Cord's helmet, knocking it askew as he turned away. "Buckle your strap."

With fumbling fingers, Cord fastened his helmet in place, while his teacher reached into his pocket.

Lopez waved a business card in front of his face. "You should take my fall class in Colorado."

Cord's already racing heart jumped up a notch. "You really think I can be a professional bull rider?"

"Not a chance!" Lopez's shoulders shook with laughter. "Besides being a decade too late, I'm afraid you don't have the natural talent."

"Then why should I take your class?"

"Because you have what it takes…" Lopez paused and tapped the card in Cord's frozen fingers. "You have the guts to be a bull *fighter*."

Cord's eye dropped to read the words, printed in bold letters, "Colorado Rodeo School: Professional Bullfighter Training." The card burned his fingers like a hot coal.

"You've got me all wrong. I'm not even sure I can make myself get on a bull when he's pinned in a chute."

"You're afraid, and you should be. But you'll do it."

"That's because I'm depending on my speed to get away from him when he bucks me off."

Cord had done his research before coming to the class. An internet article had explained how Lopez had retired from bull riding to become a bullfighter, supposedly inspired by another bullfighter who was critically injured saving Lopez from almost certain death. Cord had shuddered at the story, certain an experience like that would've convinced him never to step foot in an arena with a bull.

His father would've done it, though. He'd been fearless, even as a kid. Uncle Dave had told Cord at least fifty times how his dad had spotted a copperhead snake just before Dave stepped on him. As he'd yelled and pushed his younger brother out of the way, he'd been bitten by the venomous snake, leading to a two-week stay in the hospital.

But Cord was nothing like his heroic father. "There's no way I could run *toward* an angry, bucking bull." He tried to hand the business card back to Lopez.

"You could do it if you had to." Lopez shrugged and pushed Cord's hand back. "Keep it, in case you change your mind."

Cord slid the card into his back pocket, determined to throw it away at his earliest opportunity.

6

"*Y*ou're really going through with this?"

Cord's weekly conversation with Finn had centered more on the upcoming rodeo than his progress on the new software program. With his right arm in a sling, Cord could only use his left hand to steer as he made his daily commute to Sage Valley Ranch.

"I can't back out."

"You rode a bull. Haven't you already proven yourself?"

"It's something I have to do." Cord's chest was so tight, he could barely breathe. Could he really tell someone how he felt without breaking down? "Because of my dad."

"Was he a rodeo bull rider?"

"No, but he was a real cowboy. Tough as nails. He never criticized, but I think he was disappointed when my best friend was in rodeo competitions and I wasn't."

"He had to be proud of you," said Finn. "Look what you've accomplished."

"He didn't express his emotions a lot. I think he was

proud, but kind of disappointed I didn't want to be a rancher, like him."

"You're still grieving. You should be careful making lifechanging decisions."

"I will." Cord's throat felt like someone had their hands around it, squeezing with all their might. With a force of will, he bundled his sudden emotions and pushed them back inside—the guilt, the grief, the self-reproach.

Every decision he'd ever made was suspect. The time he'd lost with his father while living in New York the last nine years filled him with regret. What choices would he have made if he'd known his dad was going to die so young? For the most part, he couldn't go back and redo his life decisions… except for this rodeo.

"I can't help wondering what might've happened if I'd stayed closer to home. I feel like I ran away from everything Sage Valley represented. Riding in this rodeo is me facing it head on."

"Taking the proverbial bull by the horns?" asked Finn.

"Ha! I guess so."

"If you're determined to do this, I'll support you. And… I'm coming to watch."

IT WAS times like these Jess really missed having her roommate to talk to. Why did Laurel have to be on a mission trip this summer in a remote area of Zimbabwe, of all places? Why couldn't she have picked a place with cell and internet service?

Lexi's advice to share her true feelings plagued Jess, repeating itself like a tolling bell in her mind. But Jess didn't trust her fleeting emotions. She preferred to keep a safe distance until she knew this was something more than infatuation. No use ruining a perfectly good friendship.

With no one else she wanted to spill her guts to, Jessica attempted to handle the issue on her own. She rehearsed an untold number of possible scenarios in her mind. Late into the night she held imaginary conversations with Cord. By the time she arrived at breakfast Monday morning, she felt ready to face him and maintain her composure in front of her grandparents. Of course, the real discussion couldn't take place until they found a place to speak in private, but she'd even practiced those dialogues so she could speak her mind without letting her emotions clog her brain.

She waited for Cord to appear, chewing her biscuit slowly so her plate wouldn't be empty when he arrived. But nothing could've prepared her for the moment when Cord stepped foot through the kitchen door. Her guts rolled like the ocean as she took in his injuries.

"Cord!" Nanna gasped, a fist raised to her open mouth. "What happened to you?"

He sank slowly into a chair at the table, as if his pockets were stuffed with raw eggs. His dark-framed glasses did nothing to hide a black and purple eye. A swollen lip accompanied the scratches on his face. His bandaged right hand protruded from a sling. Altogether, he looked like he'd had a fight with an eighteen-wheeler.

"You should see the other guy." His chuckle turned into

a wince, and he sucked in a sharp breath. "Ow. It hurts to laugh."

"You were in a fight?" Jessica tried to slow her racing heart, pressing a hand on her chest.

He shook his head, flinching again. "No, that was a joke."

Her grandfather peered over the top of his paper. "Did you get in a wreck?"

"I might as well confess, since I can't hide it." Cord's sigh was long and heavy. "I was practicing for the rodeo."

"Oh my gosh," Jess exclaimed. "Did you break anything?"

"Dislocated my right shoulder. Sprained some fingers. Other than that, it's mostly bruises. I might've broken a few ribs," he said, as if his injuries were no big deal. "Nothing that'll keep me from riding in the ranch rodeo."

"Is that why you're wearing glasses today?" asked Nanna.

"Yeah. This eye can't handle a contact right now."

"You know, Cord… maybe you shouldn't compete in the ranch rodeo."

Nanna took the words right out of Jessica's mouth. But Cord's hurt expression made her glad she hadn't expressed the sentiment.

"Bull riding is a rough sport," he said, jutting out his chin. "Injuries are part of the game."

"He's right," said Bucky, once again buried behind his newspaper. "That's bull riding for you."

Unbidden images rushed into Jessica's head. Cord, bucked into the air and falling to the ground in a heap. A wildly bucking bull landing with both hooves on Cord's back, snapping his spine.

Gruesome! What's wrong with me?

Though she'd always loved to watch bull riding in the past, her imagination was going haywire. The possibility of Cord getting trampled by a thrashing bull had her stomach threatening to expel her freshly eaten biscuit. Suddenly, she needed some air.

"I've got to go," she mumbled, leaping to her feet, her chair legs scraping the tile floor.

"You didn't finish eating," said Nanna.

"I'm full, Nanna," she said, scrambling to open the door. "Thanks for breakfast."

"Wait," Cord's voice called as she slammed the door shut, but she ignored him, sucking in lungsful of fresh air until her queasy gut calmed.

How could she be so upset about Cord in a bull riding competition, after watching her own brother compete for years?

Must be this stupid diet I started. Too much spinach. Not enough chocolate. My system's totally out of whack.

She jumped as the door opened behind her and Cord limped out.

"Hey," he said. "Can we talk?"

Even with a black eye and a swollen lower lip, he was handsome, but she couldn't bring herself to look at him.

"I need to check on Shadow," she said, twisting the ring on her pinky finger.

"It'll only take a minute. We could sit on the swing."

The comfy white porch swing beckoned, swaying in the

morning breeze. But swinging together meant having a deep conversation. Last night she'd decided to tell him everything, but now, with her frazzled emotions hanging by a thread, she'd lost her nerve. Maybe she could keep the talk light and playful.

"Okay," she answered. "At least I don't have to worry about you kissing me."

"Was that a challenge?" His lips formed a swollen half-grin.

"No." She tried to frown, but failed. "You can joke all you want, but you're still in trouble."

"I am?" He eased himself onto the contoured wood slats with minimal wincing, and she sat beside him, a comfortable six inches between them as the swing began to move. "You mean I got all these injuries for nothing? I thought you might not want to murder me if I already looked half dead—battered and bleeding."

"You see, that's where you messed up. Battered doesn't get any sympathy. Bleeding would've done it, but you already stopped the blood flow."

"Darn. I'd have sacrificed the truck upholstery if I'd known." He pushed his glasses up with his unbandaged hand. "I should've said this before, but I'm sorry I kissed you in front of all those guests."

"It was pretty embarrassing."

"I know. I wish I could make it up to you."

For a few brief seconds, they sat in contented silence, enjoying the peaceful moment. A gentle morning breeze ruffled her hair as the cicadas sang their dissonant song. Then a brilliant idea sprang into her mind.

"I know how you can make it up to me. Promise you won't compete in the bull riding."

Anger clouded his face. "You're okay with Mason McCaffrey riding, but you think I'm too much of a wimp to ride?"

Maybe it wasn't such a brilliant idea.

"That's not it at all."

"Really?" He stopped the swing, glaring at her. "Then why don't you want me to compete?"

How could she explain her severe anxiety without making it seem like an insult?

"Because you're already injured."

It seemed like a good argument, until he answered, "Your brother once competed with a broken hand, and everyone said he was tough. All I've got are broken ribs."

"Go ahead and ride, then," she said, hating the wobble in her tone. "Kill yourself, if that's what you want. It's none of my business."

"That's right. It isn't." He turned his head, staring ahead, muscles flexing along his jaw.

"Fine." Acid churned in her stomach. It definitely wasn't fine. "If your life isn't my business, then mine isn't yours, either."

He snapped his face toward her. "Meaning?"

"Meaning, you and my brother need to stay out of my business."

"You're the one who pulled me into this mess last Thursday with that crazy story about us going to the dance together. All I did was try to make your lie look believable."

Guess that clarifies how he feels about me. No use baring my soul. Especially when it's probably a fleeting attraction, instead of love.

"You're officially off the hook. We'll tell everyone we're not dating."

"And what about McCaffrey?"

"Not your problem. I shouldn't have made up that *crazy story*." She sat forward, preparing to escape before she blurted out something she would regret.

"Wait! Don't go." His hand touched her arm. "I'm sorry I said that."

"No need to apologize. It's the truth."

"No, it's not." He cleared his throat, swallowing audibly. "The truth is… when that whole fiasco started, I was on my way to ask you to the dance."

Her breath caught in her throat. What was he saying? Then she remembered his motivation.

"I don't need a date to the dance. Tell Nick I can take care of myself." Blinking at unexplained tears, she surged out of the swing, aiming her feet toward the stables.

But Cord followed on her heels, albeit with a few moans of pain. "It had nothing to do with Nick. I was planning to invite you because I *like* you."

Stunned, she stopped in her tracks, and he moved to stand in front of her. The air grew so thick, she couldn't get it into her lungs. With shallow breaths, she studied his well-worn boots, mostly to avoid his gaze.

"It's possible I actually wanted you to ask me." Her pulse raced. Had she actually said that out loud?

"How possible is possible?"

"I'm guessing seventy percent. Maybe seventy-one."

His head bent low, and she spied his swollen smile. The scratches didn't hide his dimples. "I'll take those odds. They're way better than my chance of making eight seconds."

His hand reached for hers, but she tucked it safely in her back pocket. "I can't date anyone right now. Not until I graduate."

He made a strangled sound. "That's almost a year from now."

She risked a quick glance and saw him push his hand through his dark hair, his brows bent with frustration.

"We could be friends." She tried to make it sound like a great compromise.

"Friends." He rubbed the scruff of beard on his face. "Does your definition of friends include kissing?"

"No," she choked, swallowing a lump of air.

"How about dinner? Walks? Horse rides? Picnics?"

His boots scooted closer, and she took a step back.

"That sounds an awful lot like dating."

"Not necessarily," he said. "I've done all those things with friends. Haven't you?"

"I guess so."

"What if I bought you an ice cream bar? Right now?"

A grin fought its way onto her face. "Then I might like you seventy-*two* percent."

His hand beckoned again. "We can hold hands. Friends do it all the time."

"I don't think we should." His touched affected her too much. She might lose control.

"It'll keep McCaffrey off your back." His enticing fingers wiggled.

Against her better judgment, she slipped her hand into his large, masculine grasp, straining to remain still when sparks shot through her nerves. His hand tugged, leading her toward the ranch store, their boots crunching the oak tree acorns along the path.

"I have a confession to make," he said, as he limped along beside her. "I lied."

"About what?"

"I was never sorry about kissing you."

Her mouth opened, ready to spout a sharp comeback, but not a single thing came to mind.

7

"*I*t's called *Orange Zest.* I know it feels weird, but I think you're going to love it. It makes you look very bright and cheery."

No reply came from Jessica's toes, wedged apart with a blue foam separator.

"You probably don't remember, but you wore it all the time last summer. I've been neglecting you since you're almost always hidden in boots."

Pressed for time, Jess tried to rush on the next foot, painting a bit more than the nail on her big toe. She used a tissue to rub off the excess, but it left the skin discolored.

"Great—now you look injured, and I don't have any polish remover."

She could borrow some remover from her grand-mother, but then she'd get a thorough inquisition about why she was painting her toenails. She was hoping to sneak out of the house without being seen. Living in the main house, rather than the bunk room with the other staffers, had major advantages, like the entire upstairs to herself, along with access to the upstairs wraparound screen porch. But along with a private bedroom, private bathroom, and private breakfast came a not-so-private social life. "Sorry, toe. You're just going to have to be orange, like your nail."

Jess stood and hobbled to the bed, where she'd laid her outfit for the evening—one of only two dresses she'd included in her hurried packing for the summer at the dude ranch. Though she was excited about going to dinner at The Cabernet, the nicest restaurant in Sage Valley, she worried it was a bad idea to do something so date-like. It was one thing to eat ice cream together. She'd insisted on buying one for him the next day, to cement the *friendship* aspect of the relationship. They'd finished out the week with a daily ice cream bar, alternating who picked up the tab. But she didn't have the funds to reciprocate in kind for a dinner like this.

"I have more money, so I can afford a nice dinner," Cord had argued, as he pulled the wrapper down on his ice cream sandwich. "It doesn't mean anything."

She should've turned him down when he invited her that morning, but a chance to eat at her favorite restaurant was too tempting.

"It makes me nervous," she'd said, coughing as she moved to her left, giving a blessed inch of separation between their legs as they sat on the iron bench under the tree in front of the general store.

An impudent smile had slid onto his face, a bit crooked from the lingering swelling on his lip. "Nervous looks cute on you."

His hand had lifted, moved slowly toward her face, and tucked a stray strand of hair behind her ear. The gesture had felt so intimate, her cheeks had burned, along with something deep in her gut. She'd licked the outside of her fudgesicle to catch a drip and taken a bite, with a vain hope it would cool her off, inside and out.

"Don't touch me like that." Her objection had sounded ridiculous. After all, they'd held hands each day when walking to their ice cream outings, even though Mason was no longer acting aggressive. Jess gave a lame explanation. "It tickles."

His mouth had twitched, and she'd wondered if he was somehow reading her mind. He'd leaned closer, his warm breath feathering her ear. "Would you rather I kissed you?"

"No," she'd lied, her grip tightening on her fudgesicle stick. "We're friends, only. You promised not to push me."

"I never said anything about pushing you. My exact words were *I promise not to kiss you.*" Then his brows had waggled behind his glasses. "But I didn't promise to resist if *you* decide to kiss *me.*"

She'd gulped a lump of air. "Then I think we shouldn't go to The Cabernet tonight."

"Does that mean my plan is working? Are you afraid if we go out to a nice dinner, you won't be able to stop yourself? One bite of juicy end-cut prime rib and you'll lose control and throw your arms around my neck and kiss me senseless?"

"No, of course not—" She'd stopped, as his words sunk in. "End-cut prime rib?"

"You told me it was your favorite. I called yesterday and paid in advance so they would save it for you."

Her mouth had watered. He'd gone to a great deal of trouble to ensure she would get one of the two end pieces off the prime rib. Had anyone ever gone to such lengths to please her before? Certainly not Parker. It would've been rude to turn Cord down when he'd made such a sweet gesture, right? She'd just have to make sure they sat on opposite sides of the table so there was no inadvertent contact between them.

She stared into the mirror and shook her finger at her eager-eyed reflection. "Tonight must be completely platonic. No flirting. And definitely no kissing. If the thought even crosses your mind, think about something else, like... *going to the dentist!*" A great big needle and the whir of the drill ought to chase away any thoughts of locking lips with Cord.

With that settled in her mind, she hurried to finish getting ready. At least she'd managed to talk Holden into leading the evening trail ride so she had time to shower and shave her legs. She donned the green sundress, lamenting that her arms had turned dark, despite religious use of sunblock. "White shoulders, tanned arms, and an orange toe. At least I'll be colorful."

Her grandparents' voices drifted from the family room up the stairwell as she tiptoed down, in hopes of escaping unnoticed. Two steps from the bottom, the board under her foot emitted a loud creak.

Heat flashed up Jessica's neck the moment her grandmother's head turned, her sharp gaze zeroing in.

"You're all dressed up tonight," Nanna said. "Where are you headed?"

"Just out with friends, Nanna." Jess moved off the stairs and continued toward the kitchen.

"Would that friend happen to be Cord Dennison? I heard the two of you are dating, now."

With a groan, Jess returned to the family room. She perched in a chair opposite the couch, her hopes of a quick conversation dashed when Bucky clicked off the television, to give Jess his undivided attention, along with Nanna.

"Cord and I aren't dating. We're only friends."

"Hmmm." Nanna wore an expression like she was talking to a snake-oil salesman. "That's not what Mason McCaffrey told us."

"What is he, a middle-schooler? Tattling to my grand-parents just because he's jealous?"

"Actually, he assumed you'd already told us." Bucky leaned forward, resting his elbows on his knees. "He and one of the summer staffers came by to let us know they were dating and to sign a policy awareness form."

"Oh." Her bluster gone, Jess scrunched her polish-adorned toes, still resenting the intrusion. "I kind of forgot about the employee dating policy thing. Besides, we really are keeping it in the friend zone."

"Even so, if the two of you are spending time alone together, you need to sign the form," said Bucky. "I just happen to have one right here."

Bucky handed her a piece of paper, and she read the title. *Sexual Harassment Awareness Form.* She was quite certain thinking about this form while she was with Cord would cool her off about as well as thinking about the dentist.

"But you don't have to tell us anything else about your life," Nanna said, stiffly. "Though it might be nice to know if you'll be coming in really late, since I'm a light sleeper."

Bucky coughed, smiling behind his hand.

"What?" Nanna snapped. "I *am* a light sleeper."

"You could sleep through a twenty-one-gun salute," said Bucky, with a chuckle.

Jess knew her grandmother's feelings were hurt. "I'm sorry I didn't say anything about Cord, Nanna, but I didn't want to get your hopes up for nothing. We're going out as friends, and that's all."

Nanna's stony expression softened. "You just need to listen to your heart, Jess."

"That's what got me engaged to Parker. This time, I'm listening to my head, and my head is telling me, *absolutely no dating*."

Cord slid around the turn in a spray of dust and gravel and came to a stop in front of the Buchanan's white clapboard house. He hadn't intended to be late, but he'd been halfway back to Sage Valley Ranch when he realized he'd forgotten his deodorant. Returning to apply the protection had cost an extra fifteen minutes, but he wouldn't have dared the date without it.

He leapt from the truck, ignoring the searing pain in his left knee, and hurried up the stone path, hoping his deodorant was up to the task. He was almost as nervous about talking to Jessica's grandparents as he was about the date. Not that Jessica called it a date, but that was his intent.

Tonight, he would show her his sophisticated side. Despite growing up in a small country community, Jessica liked big cities, now. If Jess liked big city life, he would show it to her, right there in Sage Valley.

He, of all people, could understand the appeal of the city. Hadn't he been living out his dream in New York City for the past nine years? And the door wasn't closed, yet. Finn was still determined to keep him at Phantom Enterprises.

But every day he heard his father's haunting question. *"Son, I just want to know one thing, and I can die in peace. Are you happy?"*

When his dad first asked the question, Cord had been shaken to the core. Not because his dad asked it, but because it was the first time he'd ever seen his dad cry. Cord had assured him he was happy. He had everything he'd ever wanted. A successful career. The respect of his peers. A bright future in an exciting city. Lots of friends. A great life.

Yet Cord saw his parents' friends, who brought food, sat at the hospital, took over the work on the ranch, raised money to help with hospital bills, and wept with the family when his father finally died. It seemed something about the small community of Sage Valley drove the bonds of friendship deeper. What Cord had once viewed as people being-in-your-business, he now saw as compassion and caring.

He couldn't help wondering what he'd been running from nine years ago. And his father's question echoed unanswered in his head.

Cord limped up the steps, still favoring his sore knee. Clad in a custom-tailored suit, he ought to feel confident in his appearance. But even though he'd opted to forgo the sling on his arm, he couldn't look too sophisticated sporting a black eye.

He knocked on the door, surprised when Jess answered with an anxious expression.

"Hi, Cord. I—" Her jaw dropped. "Wow, you look great." Her hands smoothed her dress down. "I think I'm underdressed."

His gaze dropped, taking in the pretty dress and the shapely calves it exposed. "No. You're perfect. Absolutely perfect."

She graced him with a shy smile, pink rising to her cheeks. Then she whispered, "I hate to ask, but can you come in for a minute?"

"Sure. I've got something for your grandfather." He whipped the folded papers from his coat pocket. "You're going to need to fill one of these out, too. It's kind of awkward, but Sage Valley Ranch requires us to—"

"Sign a Sexual Harassment Awareness form," she finished with him. "I know. I just did it. Signed it with my own blood."

He laughed, relieved someone else had broken the news to her. "I used ink. Hope it's still valid."

As he entered, Bucky stood to greet him, his brows

rising as he looked him over. "Evening, Cord. Is this how you New Yorkers dress?"

"My last job required me to wear a suit every day, so I have quite a few." He held the form out, a sudden bout of nerves making his hand shake. "I've already filled out my form. And I want you to know this is our first official date."

"It's not a date," Jessica mumbled, behind his back.

Bucky scanned the form. "It's been a long time since a boy came to take one of my daughters on a date. I don't even know what's proper anymore. Do I ask where you're going or what time you'll have her home?"

Cord heard Jess grumbling behind him and waved his hand at her behind his back. "You can ask anything you like, Mr. Buchanan."

Nanna appeared at Bucky's side, taking his arm. "You don't ask them anything, Bucky. Cord is a fine young man, and Jess is a grown woman. She's been supporting herself for the last four years. I'm sure Cord will take her someplace nice and have her home at a decent time, like any gentleman would."

Behind him, his hand was tugged, dragging him backwards toward the door. "I'll have her home by midnight," he promised, in a loud voice to cover Jessica's mutterings.

"I can't believe him," she snapped, the moment the door closed behind them. "So embarrassing."

Their fingers interlocked as they walked to the truck, and he noted how well their hands fit together. "I think it's kind of nice," he remarked. "I mean, other than the fact that I felt like a nervous teenager, it's nice that they care so much. Bucky didn't mean any harm."

"You're right." Her jaw protruded in a stubborn way he was beginning to expect. "But it's hard to be under their thumb when I'm used to being on my own. Nothing gets past Nanna."

He opened her door and helped her into the truck. "Sorry you have to climb up in a dress. Living in New York, I don't even own a car. When I came home, Dad let me use his truck. Her name's Charlene... Charlene, the Chevy."

"I always think of cars as females and trucks as males," Jess said, patting the dashboard. "Rough and rugged."

"This truck is definitely female. Very moody. Won't even start when it's cold."

"Are you kidding me? Guys are plenty moody," she said, as she latched her seatbelt.

"Charlene is kind of beat up on the outside," he said in apology. "Our other truck is newer, but it's a standard. My shoulder hurts when I shift gears."

"Don't worry. I'm not a car snob. My truck has almost 200,000 miles on it."

"So does Charlene, but Dad kept her in great shape."

And now he's gone.

Without warning, Cord's throat tightened. He quickly shut her door and turned his back to hide the moisture that sprang to his eyes. He'd held it together for the months during his dad's illness, burying his emotions deep inside. Even after his father's death, he'd successfully avoided any emotional outbreaks. Why was he falling apart now, of all times? After a few calming breaths, he moved around to the driver's side and scrambled in, a cumbersome task without the use of his right arm.

He gripped the steering wheel with his left hand and forced a smile on his face. "Ready to go eat?"

"Would you rather go somewhere and talk?" she asked, in a soft voice.

He must not have turned his face away in time. Her gentle touch on his arm was almost enough to make him lose control and blubber like a baby. His hands shook as he held on by a thread. He couldn't bring himself to look at her, but he knew her expression was full of pity. Somehow, he had to distract her.

Bending awkwardly, he turned the key with his left hand, and the engine revved to life. "Let's talk on the way to dinner. We'll talk about how beautiful you are tonight."

She took the bait. "Maybe we should talk about how I smeared nail polish, and I now I have a bright orange toe."

"Yep, that neon toe was the first thing I saw when you opened the door."

"It was?"

A glance showed her horrified expression.

"I'm teasing, Jess. I wouldn't have noticed if you'd painted your entire foot. I was too busy looking at your legs."

She laughed, light and musical, and he felt like he'd won a prize.

"I want to put in a request," he said. "You'd make me very happy if you'd wear shorts every day, instead of blue jeans."

"I may have to report that to my grandfather," she

replied, with a chuckle. "What you just said could be construed as sexual harassment."

"That suggestion was made purely with your health in mind. Uncovering those shapely legs would make you less likely to have a heat stroke in the Texas sun. Nothing sexual in that."

"You were thinking of my health, huh? What if I suggested you walk around the ranch without a shirt, for the same reason?"

"I'd say, be careful what you ask for."

His eyes were on the road, but he felt her skeptical glower.

"You wouldn't dare," she said.

"How about a bet? I'll go shirtless if you wear shorts all day."

"It's not a fair trade. You'll just do paperwork and stay inside. My job is mostly outside, working with the horses."

"No, I'll walk around outside. I'll even show up at breakfast without a shirt, though I doubt your grandmother will let me in her kitchen if I'm indecent."

"The whole day? Inside and out?"

He nodded, wondering how he would pull it off. "Seven a.m. to five p.m."

"You've got a deal," she said, her huge grin showing off perfect white teeth.

She stuck out her hand, and he shook it, wincing at the sharp pain in his shoulder. Without the sling, he'd momentarily forgotten the injury.

"There should be some kind of penalty if you don't make it the whole day," she added.

"How about if one of us doesn't make it the whole day, we have to buy the ice cream for a week?"

"No, that's too easy." She tapped a fingernail on her front tooth. "How about this? You have to tell me something you've never told anyone... anything I want to know."

With that threat looming, Cord would be willing to walk around in his underwear. There was no way he'd lose. "Okay, but the same applies to you. And your shorts have to be actual shorts—above your knees—not those short pants that only show your ankles."

"Agreed." She chuckled, shaking her head.

"What are you laughing at?"

"I'm pretty sure this whole conversation violated that agreement we signed."

"No, it didn't. It was all about preventing heat stroke, remember? Texas in the summer? 101 degrees in the shade?"

"Right. I forgot," she said, still grinning.

After a moment, his stomach clenched. "But seriously, Jessica, if I ever said anything that made you feel... objectified or put down or disrespected..."

"Don't worry, Cord. I don't think you'd ever do that," she said, her expression somber. "But if you did, I'd let you know. And the same goes for me."

He reached his hand out and, after a moment's hesitation, her fingers interlaced with his.

So far, this date is going really well.

They drove a few miles in silence and he let his thumb explore the soft skin on her hand with gentle strokes.

Maybe tonight, he could make her realize how silly it was for them to put off their relationship. Pretending to only be friends was a ridiculous idea. A glance showed his ministrations were having the desired effect. Head back, eyes closed, rapid breaths.

Yes, it's working. I am a master!

"Have you ever had a shot in your mouth?" she asked, out of the blue.

"Huh?"

"I was sitting here, thinking about when I had to have a cavity filled last year. One of my sealants came out. Have you ever had a cavity filled?"

"A couple, but it's been a while." Confused, he withdrew his hand. "I think I was fourteen."

"Do you floss?"

"Uhmm… sometimes. Not as often as I should."

"It's really important to prevent gum disease."

Smooth, Dennison. You rubbed her hand and made her think about the dentist.

8

When Monday morning arrived, Jessica was ready to win the bet. Cord thought she would chicken out, but she was way too competitive to do that. She had to win. She absolutely had to. Especially after dinner Friday night.

To call her plan to use dental appointments to take her mind off Cord's magnetism ineffective would be an understatement. A huge one. Bigger than the Milky Way. Bigger than the pile of laundry falling out of her overstuffed hamper.

By the time they'd finished their prime rib and dessert, and Cord had driven her home and walked her to the door, she'd recounted every single dental experience she could remember in graphic detail. Including the time, while under the lingering influence of drugs from her wisdom-tooth extractions, she'd told her oral surgeon he was "dreamy." But no dental description—whether frightening, funny, or downright gory—could compete with Cord's allure. If only he would stop caressing her fingers with those devious hands of his. One thing was certain, his professed plan to make her want to kiss him, and thus circumvent her friends-only rule, was working. So far, she'd hidden that fact from him, but how long could she hold out?

She was terrified she was racing down the same path she'd gone with Parker. Especially since Cord was even more attractive than her ex. Though she had to admit, as opposed to Parker, Cord Dennison seemed both thoughtful and respectful, not to mention, romantic.

But their relationship was doomed from the start. She'd already determined she wanted nothing to do with city life. She'd even arranged to do her student teaching at Sage Valley High, though she hadn't broken the news to Nick, yet. Her other brothers would never interfere, but Nick acted like a controlling mother.

Yet as much as she now wanted to come back home after college, she found herself considering whether she might throw away her own aspirations so she could be with Cord. Hadn't she been the same way with Parker? That had red warning signs all over it—flashing, with horns and sirens.

That's why she was gung ho about this shorts-and-shirt-less challenge. It was fun, required no physical contact, and rested squarely in the friend-zone. She and Laurel had pulled similar harmless pranks at UNT.

Jessica clomped down the stairs, already self-conscious in her shorts and boots. Though she'd seen other girls wearing similar outfits—western style boots with shorts or dresses—Jess thought it looked ridiculous. Maybe she could pull it off with some cute fashionable boots instead of old, well-worn and twice-resoled cowboy boots, but she didn't own any.

Not that it mattered. As soon as Cord showed up at breakfast with his shirt on, she could declare victory. She figured at most, she'd have to get through the morning trail ride before switching to back to jeans. But she was positive he didn't have the guts—or maybe it would be the stupidity —to show up for breakfast at Nanna's without a shirt. She'd made it clear breakfast was part of the bargain, and she wouldn't let him off the hook.

"Morning, Nanna. Yum! Do I smell bacon?"

"Yes, I have bacon in the oven. Eggs are almost done, and I have homemade tortillas."

"Breakfast tacos! I've died and gone to heaven."

"Well, you can thank Cord."

"Why?"

"He called yesterday and made a special request. Said he's got something special going on today and wondered if he could get breakfast to go."

"Oh, no you don't," Jess muttered under her breath, her fists tightening. She couldn't let him get around the terms of the agreement.

"What'd you say?" Nanna asked.

"I said… uhmm…. 'too bad you won't…'" Her mind worked fast. "Too bad you won't insist he comes in for breakfast, no matter what he says. He told me sometimes he feels like he's taking away your private family time.

That's probably why he asked for breakfast to go. He thinks you're too polite to tell him he's imposing."

"Of course he's not imposing." From Nanna's aghast expression, one would've thought Jess had suggested putting the dog down.

Just then, the door cracked open and Cord's face jutted inside. "Hi, Sharon. I'm here for that breakfast taco."

Jess dashed to the door and flung it open, exposing a shirtless-Cord, with a pair of bright blue swim trunks hanging from his hips and a life vest slung over his left shoulder. Much to her disappointment, his arm sling blocked her view of his chest. Yet she could still discern his broad shoulders and muscular arms and legs.

What's he been doing in New York City? Lifting taxicabs with his bare hands?

He grinned at her, a glint of triumph in his eyes, and she scowled.

"That sling covers almost as much as a shirt," she said, lowering her voice.

His smile only broadened as he whispered back, "You said *no shirt*. You didn't say *no sling*."

"But you have to have breakfast with Nanna and Bucky, not grab it to go."

"No, you only said I had to show up for breakfast without a shirt on, and I did." He smirked, calling out, "Sharon, is that breakfast taco ready?"

"Not quite," came Nanna's reply. "Come on in and have a seat. I'll have it ready in a jiffy."

His smile faltered on one side as he yelled back, "I'd

love to, Sharon, but I'd better not. You don't want me coming in, dressed the way I am."

"I don't care how you're dressed, Cord Dennison. I'll be offended if you don't eat with us. Jessica told me what you said, and I want you to know, you're absolutely not imposing."

Jessica pressed her hand over her mouth to keep her laughter inside.

His eyes narrowed to slits, flashing blue lightning bolts at Jess. Jaw clenched, he squeezed between his teeth, "What did you say to her?"

"No idea what she's talking about." Jess blinked her wide-open eyes, feigning innocence. "It's only fair. If I'm going to be humiliated all day, you at least have to experience a little embarrassment at breakfast."

"Don't worry. I'll have plenty of humiliation." He flung his left hand in a wild gesture toward the watersports trailer, where staffers were already loading canoes and kayaks for the morning trips. "I'll be standing around the river all day, practically useless, unless I'm willing to risk reinjuring my shoulder to carry boats to the river or use a paddle. And I'd look like an idiot wearing this life vest while I'm standing on the bank, so I'll be answering questions all day about these…"

He turned around, and she gasped at the sight of his back and sides, covered with blue and greenish bruises.

"Oh Cord! That looks terrible!" Had he simply been bucked off the bull, or had he been kicked in the ribs a few hundred times? He didn't look in the mood to answer questions.

"And all you have to do is show off your legs a bit." His gaze dropped down, and he let out a low whistle, closing his eyes as if the sight was too much for him. Her cheeks burned like she was sitting too close to a bonfire. "Dang, Jess. I'm a sucker for girls with muscular calves. I'm almost ready to concede defeat just to keep Holden and Mason from ogling your legs all day."

"Fine by me," she said, extending her hand. "Declare me the winner, and I'll run upstairs and change back into jeans."

In the sling, his right hand twitched, his brow furrowing. He was thinking about it. Jess might win the bet without setting foot from the house.

"Cord," Nanna called. "Are you coming to breakfast?"

The smell of bacon wafted out the door, and Cord's stomach gave an eager growl. A slow smile bloomed on his face.

"I'm coming, Sharon."

Cord stepped past Jess into the kitchen, and her hopes of a quick victory plummeted. He flashed a grin over his shoulder and mouthed, "I win."

She couldn't help grinning back as she came close and muttered, "The day's not over."

DROPPING his life jacket beside the door, Cord steeled himself for Sharon's reaction. When she turned around her jaw dropped to the floor, and the panful of bacon in her hands almost followed suit.

"Oh!" Her mouth opened and closed like a guppy. "I didn't realize... I mean..."

"Sorry, Sharon. I'm working down at the river today. I didn't plan to come inside, so I don't have a shirt." He backed toward the door. "I'll just wait outside for one of those breakfast tacos. I really appreciate it."

Sharon frowned. "Nonsense. You'll sit right down at that table and eat your breakfast. I may not have had any sons, but it's not like I've never seen a man's chest before."

"But what about your sign?" He pointed to her refrigerator, which was littered with snappy messages, like *In this kitchen, we lick the spoon*, and *A messy kitchen is a happy kitchen*. One sign was prominent, front and center... *No shirt, no shoes, no service*.

She waved him toward the table. "Forget those kitchen magnets. Only one sign matters." She pointed to the wall, where a hand-painted wood sign read, *Number one rule of Nanna's kitchen: Keep Nanna happy at all times*.

With a sinking feeling, he edged sideways toward the table, hoping to hide the worst of his bruises from her sharp eyes. Next thing, she'd be asking for a copy of the doctor's report. He heard Jessica's stifled snicker and whispered, "Revenge is sweet," to which she snorted laughter.

"Why are you walking funny?" Sharon plopped the bacon on the table and fisted her hands on her hips. "Have you been riding bulls again?"

"No ma'am. Still healing from the last round." Truth was, he was afraid he was going to forget everything if he didn't practice before the big rodeo.

"Cord Dennison, what are you trying to hide?" Pot holder in hand, she marched around behind him.

"Nothing."

He quickly plopped into a chair, but the slatted back gave her an eyeful. She tsked her disapproval.

"Has the doctor cleared you for any sports activities? I don't think he'd want you canoeing this soon after your injuries."

"Now, Sharon," said Bucky, as he entered the kitchen, newspaper tucked under his arm. "I doubt Cord wants a lecture right now."

"But he'd probably *love* getting one later on," Jess added, as she carried a plate of hash brown potatoes to the table, humor dancing in her smoky gray eyes.

"Yes, please," Cord agreed. "I haven't had a good lecture since Friday night, when Jess warned me about flossing my teeth."

"Okay, I'll lay off." Sharon chuckled, good-naturedly. "That's my chair next to Bucky, Jess. Go sit next to Cord."

With wooden legs, Jess walked around to his side, her face like someone sentenced to death.

As she sank into the chair beside him, he leaned close to murmur, "Are you afraid to sit by me?"

"No," she squeaked, laying her napkin across her lap.

Seeing his prime opportunity for revenge, he scooted forward in his chair and reached for the plate of tortillas in front of him. At the same time, he let his left leg move until it pressed against her bare thigh. She jumped, and scooched her chair away from him.

After building his breakfast taco and taking a few bites,

he repeated the shifting move, this time as he reached for a napkin.

Like he'd touched her with a hot coal, Jess sprang from her chair. "Would anyone else like some orange juice?"

"No thanks," Sharon and Bucky replied, the latter from behind his newspaper.

"I'd love some juice," Cord said, plastering a benevolent smile on his face.

When she returned with two glasses of orange juice, Jess managed to move her chair a bit farther away before sitting down, just out of reach of his extended knee.

Undaunted, Cord gulped his orange juice down and stood up. "Would anyone like a glass of water?"

Bucky looked up from his paper, his eyebrows darting high. He must not have noticed Cord's lack of attire when he was sitting. "Uhmm... no thank you."

"You certainly are thirsty," Sharon observed. "Did you put too many jalapenos on there?"

"That must be it."

"Why are you working on the river trips today?" Sharon asked.

"Let's just say I wanted to increase our *visibility* in all the recreation areas." Cord looked at Jess as he made the double-entendre.

"Don't we have enough boats?" Bucky's voice came from behind his paper.

"You've got plenty of boats. But the water sports are barely mentioned on the website. I want to have an entire feature page to entice new guests."

Cord quickly filled his glass with water and returned to

the table. His eyes locked with Jessica's, her nostrils flaring a warning, and he hesitated. But he caught the ghost of a smile and knew she was enjoying the game. He moved his chair closer to hers as he sat down, pushing his knee to the side, expecting to make contact with her smooth skin. Instead, he felt cloth. What was it?

With his eyes glued to her impassive face, he used his elbow to edge his spoon off the table. It clanged as it bounced on the tile.

"Oops! Dropped my spoon." He bent down to retrieve it, looking under the table, where he spied Jessica's thigh, neatly wrapped in her napkin. Chuckling, he came up with his spoon and set it on the table with a flourish. "Well done," he murmured.

Her lips spread in a smug smile.

The game's not over yet…

"Thanks for breakfast, Sharon. I really need to be going." He downed the last of his taco.

"Wrap one up to go?" Sharon asked.

"Thanks. I'll take you up on that."

He stood and leaned across Jess as he reached for the bacon on her left, though it took a bit of contortion to do it, deliberately rubbing his bare back against her face.

"Excuse me," he said, as he sat back down.

Her face glowed liked she'd been baked in the sun, but she was fighting back a smile. "You could've asked for the bacon, instead of reaching. Were you raised in a barn?"

"Yes, but I learned a lot from the goats." He added potatoes, eggs, black beans, salsa, and sour cream before rolling up his to-go taco.

"Like how to annoy people?" she asked.

"No. I was born with that talent."

Sharon dabbed her mouth with her napkin. "Are y'all already having a lover's spat?"

"We can't have a lover's spat, Nanna. We aren't even dating. Remember?"

"Too bad," she said. "Because it's so fun when you kiss and make up."

"Nanna!"

"Thanks for the great advice, Sharon." Cord winked at her as he stood up, ready to deliver his final blow. "By the way… I scheduled a photographer to come today. He'll be here any time now to take new pictures for the website."

"Down at the river, right?" Jessica's face looked like all the blood had drained from it. "He's taking pictures for the new water sports page?"

"No, he'll be taking pictures of *all* the activities." Cord strode to the door and snatched his life vest before turning to watch Jessica's expression. "We are a *dude ranch*. I told him to take *lots* of pictures of the trail rides today."

"That sounds very nice, Cord," said Sharon.

Bucky mumbled something unintelligible, the newspaper still covering his face.

Jessica's glare made Cord glad she didn't have laser power, or he would have been shredded into unidentifiable pieces.

9

"*A*nd you won't believe what he did." Jessica clamped her phone between her head and her shoulder as she sorted through her neglected pile of clean clothes. "He got a photographer to take pictures for the website that day. Lots of pictures. There must be a thousand with me on a horse with that stupid outfit on. I was mortified."

"You knew the photographer was coming. Why didn't you just change into jeans?" At long last, Laurel had traveled to a place with cell service, and Jess was giving her bestie an earful.

"And let Cord win the bet? No way."

"After that stunt, I assume you broke up with him?"

"I can't break up with him," Jess explained. "How can we break up when we aren't dating?"

"You could stop having ice cream together every day." Laurel's voice was thick with sarcasm.

"But you know how much I like ice cream." Jess turned

on the phone's speaker setting so she could put her socks in her dresser drawer.

"Buy your own ice cream. You don't need this *Cord* guy if the other cowboy isn't bothering you. Skip breakfast and grab a protein bar like you do when we're in Dallas. Don't spend any more time with this dude if he's so awful."

"He's not really awful." Jess backpedaled, feeing bad that she'd given such a one-sided view of Cord. "He's actually super nice. He's staying here all summer to help my grandparents redo their website and accounting system, and taking a huge cut in pay to do it. Plus, you should see how sweet he is with Nanna and Bucky. And he took me to eat prime rib. And he took me dancing so we could practice before the big Sage Valley Ranch dance. He said he doesn't like dancing, but he's really smooth. And I have to admit, those muscles felt pretty good when we were slow dancing."

"*Oh. My. Gosh.*" Laurel left a space between every word. "What?"

"You're falling for him."

"No, I'm not." Jess froze, a pair of half-folded jeans in her hands.

"You're not fooling me one bit. I know you're into him. Why didn't you tell me instead of blasting him to bits?"

"I haven't fallen for him." Jessica's heart did a somersault and landed in her stomach. "We're not even dating. Bucky made us sign that employee dating form, but that doesn't mean anything."

"Of course you're dating. You're with him all the time."

"Because we both work here. That's the only reason." Jess picked up the phone and began to pace in front of her window.

"Yeah, right." Laurel's tone gave the opposite meaning to her words. "Have you kissed him?"

"Only that one time when we were putting on a show for Mason. Since then, we've only held hands. I told him I absolutely won't date anyone until I graduate."

"I don't believe you."

"It's true." Jess tried to think of something… anything that would prove it. "Just last night, he told me he was fine with us being friends."

"Really? What were his exact words?"

"Something like, 'I want you to know, when you go back to UNT, I'll wait for you. I'll try not to push you to be more than friends. And when you graduate, if you still want me, I'll be there.'"

Silence. Jess checked her cell phone screen, but the call was still connected.

"Laurel? Did I lose you?"

"You're an idiot."

"What?"

"He's in love with you."

"He barely knows me."

"Fine. Maybe he's not in love yet, but he's headed that way. Guys don't make promises about the future. That's commitment, and guys run from commitment. He wouldn't talk like that if he wasn't really into you."

"Look, I'm not going to make the same mistake I made with Parker and date a guy just because he's hot." The room suddenly felt confining, so Jess walked out onto the screened porch. "Believe me, that would be easy to do. I mean, Parker was hot, but Cord makes Parker seem like Antarctica. You should see him without a shirt on. We're talking melt-your-contacts hot. And his *eyes*. They're so blue you could swim in them. Every female guest we've had ends up flirting with him."

"And you want to scratch their eyes out?"

"Maybe," she admitted. "But I don't have to. Cord acts very professional with the guests. He said he wants me to know he's not playing games."

"Good gravy, Jess!"

"What?"

"Tell him you love him. Or at least tell him you like him a lot."

"But I don't. That's what I've been trying to explain. We're just—"

"If you say the word *friends* again, I'm going to hang up right now."

"But—"

"Uh-uh. Don't want to hear it."

"Okay, I won't say it. But don't you see? When I got engaged to Parker—"

"Why do you keep going back to Parker?"

"I'm not going back. I'm learning from my past."

"Parker ruined an entire year of your life. Don't let him ruin the rest of it."

"It wasn't really Parker's fault, you know. I'm the one who put him on a pedestal and pretended he was something he wasn't."

"Jessica, you need to hear this." Laurel's heavy sigh sounded in Jessica's ear. "Parker was *controlling* and *abusive*. I never prayed for anything so hard in my life as I did for the two of you to break off that engagement."

"Why…" The room spun, and Jessica's throat swelled until she could barely speak. "Why didn't you say this before?"

"I tried. But you wouldn't listen. You had an excuse for everything he did. All the way up until you found out he wasn't really a Christian. I swear, you would've married him if he hadn't tried to make you drop your faith."

Jess remembered the moment. Parker had expressed that he went to church only because it was necessary to impress certain people.

"I guess that did open my eyes." Her voice sounded hollow.

"Thank God! I mean that, literally."

"I remember the first time I refused to do something he asked for. His face turned so purple I thought he was going to explode. But he never hit me, Laurel." Jess felt a desperate need to defend him.

"No. His abuse was verbal and emotional."

"He never tried to push me into sleeping with him. We were together nine months."

"That's because he was cheating on you the entire time," Laurel said, in a flat tone. "You ignored all the signs, but everyone knew he was doing it."

Her stomach churned, threatening to expel her dinner. She collapsed onto a white wicker chair, gasping for air like she was on top of a high mountain peak.

"He didn't yell at me." Jess knew the argument was weak.

"He didn't have to," Laurel said. "When you first went out together, he was nice. But then he started putting you down and criticizing everything that made you special. He forced you to drop out of every activity you loved and change your friends and try to be something you weren't, just to please him. And he belittled you for not doing a good enough job of changing. By the time he was finished, you were a shell of the Jessica I knew."

Jess was as stunned as if she'd been slapped in the face. It seemed as clear as day now. How could she have missed it at the time? How could she have been so weak?

"I'm even more screwed up than I realized." A terrible thought came to mind. When she whispered the words aloud, she felt like her lungs were being crushed. "Cord deserves better than me."

"Don't you dare say that." Laurel spoke like she was squeezing the last smidgeon from a tube of toothpaste. "If you believe that, Parker wins. Are you going to let that happen?"

Jess sucked air deep into her lungs and held it, then released it through her mouth in a whoosh. "No."

"That's my Jess!" Laurel let out a whoop that rang in Jessica's ear. "You're going to put this behind you and move forward with life. Now, tell me more about Cord."

As Jess answered all her roommate's questions, her mind raced, going over every detail of her relationship with Parker. How had she changed from a strong assertive woman to a weak and vulnerable version of herself?

She realized the answer. Under Parker's constant encouragement, she'd opened up and shared her deepest thoughts, believing he cared for her. He knew her secret fears and anxieties. When he began to exploit that knowledge, manipulating her emotions, she'd refused to acknowledge it.

Meanwhile, Parker hadn't shared a single vulnerable detail about himself in all that time. What she'd interpreted as his strength of character had simply been a power play.

Armed with this revelation, she questioned her judgment even more than before. She'd thought Cord and Parker were exact opposites. But just as Parker had never shared any deep, private thoughts… neither had Cord.

"BUCKY, HAVE YOU GOT A SECOND?" Cord had been wandering all over the ranch, checking every building, until he finally found Peter Buchanan repairing a hole in the chicken coop.

"Sure." He straightened and wiped his shirt sleeve across his brow, leaving a smear of dirt.

Cord shook his head, folding his page of numbers and stuffing it in his pocket. "Why don't you let me do that for you?"

"I'm not too old to do manual labor. Only seventy-four." His bushy eyebrows bent down, the dark color a stark contrast to his white hair.

Cord hoped he would be in such good shape at Bucky's age. "Yes, but you're paying me to work for you."

"I'm paying you to work on the computer stuff and the business accounting. And you're still in no shape to do strenuous work."

Bucky's gaze traveled down to Cord's arm, still tucked protectively over his sore ribs. The sling and the bandage were gone, as were most of the lacerations. From the outside, he looked fairly normal. The yellow-green was almost completely faded from the skin around his eye, and he'd abandoned his glasses for his usual contacts.

"The doc says I can start using my arm a bit." Cord didn't mention the fact that he'd been expressly forbidden from riding a bull until the dislocation was completely healed, which would take three to four months.

"A bit, huh?" Bucky's eyes narrowed, as if he wasn't quite buying the story. "What'd you want to talk about, anyway?"

"Only that I've hit a wall trying to figure out why you're losing money. At first, I thought it was McCaffrey dropping the ball, but those numbers don't add up to a huge change in income or expenses."

A chicken wandered past, stopping to pluck a bug out of the dirt.

"Be honest. Is it a lost cause?" The sudden droop of Bucky's shoulders made him look ten years older.

"No, the answer is here. Somewhere. I just need to find it. I want permission to audit all your tax records for the past six years. That way I can compare, and see what changed when your finances started going south."

"Knock yourself out," said Bucky. "I keep all the old records in the attic over the office."

"Thanks. Are you sure I can't help you with that?"

"Here's something you can do for me," said Bucky. "Hold this two-by-four at the top of this post while I secure the other end.

Glad to feel useful, Cord hefted the board with his left hand and held it in place. Bucky nailed one end with three precise strikes of the hammer, checking the level before driving a nail in the other end.

"Is the arena ready for the rodeo?" asked Bucky.

"A few minor problems, but nothing we haven't been able to handle. I think you'll be glad you added onto the grandstands. In the end, it didn't cost us any more than renting extra bleachers, and we'll be ready to go next year."

"Any other last-minute hitches?"

"Mason thinks the bullfighters we hired are a bit too inexperienced."

Bucky dug in his tool belt and extracted a nail. "That tends to be the case with the small rodeos. Everybody has to start somewhere, so we get the new guys."

"Right. Mason says not to worry. He has a plan."

"Everything will work out…" Bucky paused his sentence to hammer the last nail in place. "Just like the good Lord intended. No need to worry."

If I had that kind of faith, my stomach might not feel like I was getting an ulcer.

10

"You've been quiet tonight," Cord said, wishing he could see Jessica's expression. He had to keep his eyes on the winding country road. "Didn't you have a good time? I thought you liked dancing."

They were on their way home from the dance hall, The Two Step, where ostensibly, he'd been taking her to "practice" for the big dance. In reality, it was simply an excuse for him to hold her in his arms. She was cute as the dickens in her boots, tight jeans, and a form-fitting shirt. Tonight, her hair was pulled up in a ponytail, torturing him all night with a view of her enticing neck.

"I've been thinking," she said.

"There's your problem," he teased. "Don't you know women shouldn't think?"

He felt a soft slap on his arm, followed by a chuckle.

"Seriously, Cord, I wondered if you've ever been in love or had a serious relationship."

Cord considered her question. He'd dated a few women, but none he'd ever thought might become a permanent fixture in his life. Consumed with his education and career, to the exclusion of most everything else, he'd felt he had plenty of time to marry and start a family in his thirties. He almost told Jess he'd truly never had a relationship that would qualify as serious, but then he realized his feelings for Jess were different. Unlike the others, Jess was the kind of woman he could imagine being married to. Not that he had any intention of telling her that. He certainly wasn't ready to commit to such a thing when he couldn't make sense of his own thoughts about the future. All he knew was he wanted to date her. Really date her. Not just a couple of friends hanging out together. And as usual, he was willing to work and wait to reach his goal.

"My relationships have been fairly casual."

"Like ours?" she asked.

"Not like ours. None of those girls told me they didn't want to kiss me."

"I'm sorry." Her hand came to rest on his arm, her voice sounding stressed as she apologized. "I know I'm asking a lot, and you've been really good about it."

"It's starting to affect my ego. Makes me feel pretty rejected." He pulled his lips down like a sad puppy as he reached to take her hand.

"It has nothing to do with you, Cord. It's all me."

Keeping a straight expression, he continued his teasing. "I've heard that before. That's what women always say when they don't want to hurt your feelings. *It's not you—it's me.*" He raised the pitch of his voice to imitate a woman's.

"But I'm not just saying that," she protested. "It really is me."

To his shock, her voice trembled with emotion. She tried to withdraw her hand, but he held it tight.

"I was only playing with you, Jess. My ego isn't suffering a bit."

She shook her head like she didn't believe him. "I should never have asked you to wait a year to date me."

"You didn't ask. I volunteered. Remember?"

She sniffed, turning her face toward the window. "The truth is, you should probably just move on. I can't make promises right now. We should stop seeing each other, even as friends. It's not healthy."

"Don't say that, Jess." Cord's heartbeat skyrocketed. What was happening? Thirty minutes ago, she was melting in his arms on the dance floor. Now she was slipping away. "There's no reason we can't be friends," he argued.

"We're just kidding ourselves," she said. "We're not really friends. We don't share anything deep. We eat ice cream and go dancing, and you make me want to kiss you all the time."

"I do?" He couldn't help giving himself an internal high five.

"Yes, you do. It's awful."

"Would it be so terrible if we kissed? I thought you liked me, at least a little bit."

"I like you a lot," she whispered. "But we don't really know each other."

"Sure we do." He maneuvered down the long drive, making the left that led to her grandparents' farmhouse and stopped the truck in front of the stone walkway, killing the engine. The moonlight flooded inside, illuminating her thoughtful frown.

"Do you trust me, Cord?"

"Of course, I do. What's got you so worked up tonight?"

"I want you to answer a question, and I want you to be honest. Tell me why you're so determined to compete in the rodeo. Every time I mention it, you get mad and defensive, or you clam up."

His heart stopped beating for at least ten seconds. He wasn't ready to tell her his deepest fears. He wasn't ready to tell anyone he was afraid he would never measure up to the standard his dad had set.

With unbelievable resolve, his father had refused pain medication at the end, not wanting to miss out on his last moments with his family. Only hours before he died, he'd clasped Cord's hand, grimacing with pain. "You have to be strong, Cord. Be strong for your mom. Be strong for your sister. I'm counting on you."

Cord had made the promise, knowing it was one he could never keep. He would never be the man his dad was. Not once, the entire time his father was fighting a hopeless battle with cancer, did he complain. It wasn't surprising. The man had always been a rock—solid and dependable. He hadn't been very verbal about it, but Cord knew his dad loved him. Now he was left to fill his father's shoes, and he wasn't ready.

I never will be.

"I don't see where you have any right to criticize me

about the rodeo." He returned to a prior argument. "You're competing in the barrel racing, even though it's been two years since your last event."

"One, it's not as dangerous as bull riding. Two, Shadow and I have been practicing." She ticked off her points on her fingers. "And three, I'm not criticizing, so quit trying to make this about me."

He had one hope of distracting her without bringing his dad into the discussion.

"Is this punishment for tonight, when I got Gary to dedicate *Rootin' Tootin' Heart-Shootin' Woman* to you?"

A slideshow of emotions flitted across her face, but the one that finally settled in place was a mixture of humor and challenge. "I'm already plotting my revenge for that, even though I like that song."

"I think you look a lot like Taylor Addison," he said, hoping to keep her distracted by comparing her to the country music star who'd recorded the popular song.

Jessica's skeptical expression spelled failure. "Now I know you're full of it. I don't look anything like her."

"You're prettier," he said, and he meant it.

Her dimples peeked out, accenting those luscious lips that made it hard for him to concentrate. "Thanks. But you still haven't answered my question."

"I'd rather talk about what you said earlier."

"What's that?"

"That thing you said about wanting to kiss me?"

His joke fell flat. Her chest expanded and contracted with a huge breath and sadness settled in her eyes. "I need to go." She opened the truck door.

"Wait!" He reached to grab her elbow, but stopped himself. Something told him he shouldn't restrain her, so he begged, "Please don't leave."

She hesitated, facing away from him, one leg already hanging out the door. Her shoulders seemed to shrink into herself, making her appear small and vulnerable.

"What's this all about, Jess? We were doing fine. I haven't pushed you at all. Why are you freaking out all of a sudden?"

"I can't keep doing this, Cord. I'm starting to fall for you."

"Is that so terrible?" He swallowed hard. "I'm starting to fall for you, too."

"It's not okay." Her voice sounded tired. Resigned. "Because I'm broken."

"We're all a little broken, Jess. Life isn't easy. But you're one of the most together women I know."

"It's an act."

How could he argue with that? He knew all about putting on a brave front. "Then tell me what's wrong. Let me help you." He touched her shoulder, and she jumped like she'd been burned.

"I can't do that. Not again." She seemed to grow smaller by the second. "I'm broken because of Parker."

Slow rage built in his veins. Withdrawing his hand, he clenched his fists. He wanted to tear the man to pieces. He failed to keep an angry tremble from creeping into his voice. "What did he do to you?"

"It wasn't… it wasn't a big deal," she said. "Nothing like you're thinking. He didn't hurt me or anything."

Cord didn't believe her. "Then how did he damage you?"

She twisted to face him, her silver gaze catching his and holding it like a pinned butterfly. "How can I open up to you, if you're not willing to do the same?"

He wanted to be angry, but he saw the sincere look in her eyes. For what seemed like hours, he struggled with his warring emotions before answering, "I can't do it."

Hope vanished from her eyes like smoke in the wind. "Neither can I."

She slid out of the truck, but he jumped out, as well, falling in step beside her as she walked up to the house. Silence loomed between them until she reached the front porch.

"Jessica?"

She froze with her hand on the doorknob. "Yes?"

"I want to tell you. But I'm not ready."

Her head nodded. "You know where to find me."

The door opened and swallowed her up, closing with a heavy thunk, like the lid on a casket.

11

"Good morning, Sharon." Cord kept his eyes on the road as he answered his phone.

"I wondered if you were coming to breakfast this morning," Sharon said. "We've hardly had time to talk to you all week, what with all the extra rodeo guests."

"I do have news for you and Bucky, but it can wait until after the rodeo. Last night, I figured out what put the ranch in the red. Don't get your hopes up, but it could be a fairly easy fix. I just need to make a few phone calls on Monday."

All week Cord had buried himself in Bucky's unorganized boxes of records, which seemed to contain every single bit of correspondence that had come in the mail for the past ten years, in no particular order. In contrast, the rodeo preparations had gone off without a hitch. The advertising banners were already hanging around the arena, promoting everything from The Two Step Dance Hall to the feed store. There was even a huge sign displaying a cowboy proposing to an ecstatic girl with a wide smile and eyes to match. Evidently, the local jewelry store felt a rodeo was a romantic event.

Advertising income alone had more than covered the rodeo expenses, including the paid professionals, such as two bullfighters and a couple of off-duty police officers to keep the peace. The ranch was set to make a profit from the guests who booked rooms, not to mention their take of the tickets, plus food and drink sales, and the dance. Bucky would be able to make a hefty payment on the loan balance.

Staying up late to keep up with his Phantom Enterprise work, Cord had hardly gotten any sleep. Not that he'd have slept much anyway, replaying his last conversation with Jess.

"We've missed you at breakfast all week," said Sharon, disapproval in her tone.

"Didn't Jessica tell you why I haven't been coming?"

"As a matter of fact, she told me you two aren't seeing each other, but she didn't say what happened." Sharon left her statement hanging, an open invitation for him to spill the beans.

"I don't know if it's my place to tell you about it." Between the tax records and preparations for the rodeo event, he'd mostly avoided thinking about Jess, and he was surprised at the sharp pain in his chest. "How is she?" The question slipped out before he could stop it, like a wet spaghetti noodle sliding off a spoon.

"I don't know if it's my place to tell you about it," Sharon parroted back.

"Ouch. I guess I deserved that."

"I know you young folks think I should mind my own business, but sometimes I can't keep my mouth shut. Like this morning, for instance. Jessica got a phone call, and I thought you might want to know about it."

A ripple of apprehension had the hairs on the back of his neck standing at attention. "Who called her?"

"Parker. He'll be at the rodeo tonight."

"Why is he coming?" Blood rushed to his muscles, trembling with rage at a man he'd never met. He didn't even know what Parker had done to hurt Jess, but he knew he didn't want that weasel to talk to her.

"Parker has a way of getting what he wants," Sharon said. "And he's evidently decided he wants Jessica back."

He's not getting her.

How was Cord going to stop him? Doubtless, Jess wouldn't appreciate his interference. She'd made it clear she wanted a two-way street if they were going to talk about anything personal. And now wasn't the time to have that conversation with her.

"In case you're interested..." Sharon dangled her words like bait, "you might also like to know Jessica's taking Shadow for a ride at nine o'clock."

"If I had the time, I'd take Blaze and meet her on the trail." How could he squeeze one more thing into his day? "But with the rodeo opening tonight..."

"I understand completely, Cord. I'm sure you'll take care of what's most important." Sharon's inflection made her opinion of what qualified as *most important* perfectly clear.

SHADOW PRICKED his ears at her as she saddled him up for a morning ride, probably sensing her edginess. In part, she was nervous about the race that night. But Parker's call that morning had her rattled, to say the least. At least the trail rides were canceled for the day as the staff prepared for the two-day rodeo and the big dance on Saturday night.

"Hey, Shadow. Do you happen to be free Saturday night? I could sure use a date for the dance."

Parker announced that the engagement was officially back on, despite her protests to the contrary. If she was as strong as she hoped, she would tell him off and send him away with his tail between his legs. But Parker could be really sweet when he wanted to be. He'd spent a solid thirty minutes begging for forgiveness. He twisted her emotions, playing on her empathetic tendencies. Somehow, as he confessed how awful he'd been and proclaimed how he didn't deserve her, she found herself comforting him and telling him he was a good man.

"What's wrong with me, Shadow? Why did I tell Parker I forgave him?" she asked, as she led him out of the stable.

Jess knew a ride would be therapeutic. She could collect her thoughts and rehearse a conversation with Parker, one she hoped would be final. But what if Parker had really changed? He claimed losing her had made him reevaluate his entire life, even his opinion of church and God. She hadn't had the presence of mind to ask him what had happened to his newest girlfriend.

"It's so weird. I've been really angry with him, ever

since I talked to Laurel. But now I think I was being too hard on him. Parker actually told me he'd had it out with his mother. To me, that qualifies as opening up. It's possible he's truly changed. What do you think?"

Though Shadow never replied with words, he always seemed to make Jess feel calmer. And once they had moved up the hill and down into the open field, she let him run for a bit, enjoying the wind in her face. Nothing else mattered when she was riding. They got in a rhythm, moving together, as she balanced in the saddle. The strength of his powerful muscles seemed to flow into her body and make her feel alive.

At the far end of the field, she slowed to a walk and moved to her favorite trail that led to the river and wound along the shore. Her eyes were on a small waterfall when Shadow came to a sudden halt.

"Hi." Cord's left hand tipped his hat, his muscles flexing against a sky-blue t-shirt that matched his eyes. He looked so good her mouth watered, but she remembered their last conversation… or the lack of it. With a rigid posture, thick with tension, he sat in the saddle on a beautiful golden-red quarter horse.

"That must be Blaze." Horses had to be a safe topic. Since he kept the mare at his family's ranch home, Jess hadn't had a chance to meet her. "She's beautiful."

Cord leaned forward to stroke Blaze's neck, and Jess found herself jealous of the mare. It had only been a week, but she missed Cord's touch.

"What are you doing here?" she asked.

"We're out for a morning ride."

"Uh-huh. And you just happened to wander down this trail where Shadow and I always go."

His already deep voice dropped even lower. "It's possible I came here on purpose, hoping to run into you."

The air sparked between them. Had she ever felt like this with Parker?

"I haven't gone anywhere, Cord. You could've found me any time you liked."

"I'm here now."

"You want to talk?"

"Yes, I do." A deep furrow appeared between his brows. "I heard your ex is coming to the rodeo."

She seethed as she realized the source of his knowledge. "I'm going to kill my grandmother."

"She's only trying to help because she loves you."

"Is that so? Because I really don't see any difference between the way she tries to control me and the way Parker did it."

The second the words left her lips, she realized she'd said too much.

"Is that what he did?" The muscles worked along Cord's jaw as if he were chewing Parker to pieces. "He controlled you?"

"Maybe he did, or maybe he didn't." She clamped her mouth shut, refusing to reveal more.

"Parker has no right to make you do anything."

"Oh? Does the same go for you? Because it seems like that's exactly what you're doing. You're trying to control whether I decide to be with Parker or not."

Cord jerked his hat off, and pushed his fingers through his hair, sending it in crazy directions, but somehow looking even more delectable. "You can't go back to Parker."

"Why not?"

"Because I—" He choked on whatever he was going to say, his face turning as red as the clay on the river bank. "Because I care about you."

His sapphire eyes zoomed in on hers, piercing her soul like a laser. The entire outdoors suddenly felt too small, as if there was nowhere to hide. Heat enveloped her whole body.

"I care about you, too," she said, feeling more confused than ever.

Cord dismounted and gestured toward a fallen tree trunk beside the water. "Come sit with me."

"We don't have time. The rodeo—"

"The rodeo isn't as important as this." His fingers wiggled toward her, drawing her to him.

Even as she slid down from Shadow's back, she felt uneasy. "I don't know, Cord. I feel like Parker controlled me with words. He got into my head. And you…"

"I what?" His face was stony.

"You control me with my body. Those kisses… I can't get them out of my mind."

His lip curled up on one side, a dimple forming beside it. "What if I promise not to kiss you?"

"Even holding my hand does it," she complained.

The other side of his mouth mirrored the first, eyes crinkling in the corners. "I'm happy to hear that."

"I can't think when you touch me." She planted her fists on her hips, glaring up at him.

"Thinking is highly overrated," he rasped, his hand lifting slowly toward her face.

Her eyes closed of their own accord, and she held her breath, waiting for the white-hot sear of his fingers on her skin. But it never came. She opened her eyes and saw his face, inches away, the desire in his eyes as fierce as her own.

He straightened and turned away, his chest heaving with rapid breaths. "We're going to talk, and nothing else. I'm not going to kiss you. I'm not even going to hold your hand." The anguish in his voice sounded as if he'd pronounced his own death.

"Never mind all that," Jess hurried to assure him, flapping her hand to cool her face. "I kind of agree about thinking being overrated. In fact, I wouldn't mind a kiss right now."

"No." He stomped over and sat on the log, looking very much like a pouting school boy. "We're just going to talk. I don't want you analyzing this later and deciding I was *controlling you with your body*."

"Forget I said that." She padded along the damp path by the stream and plopped down beside him.

With a grunt, he bounced sideways, making more space between them. "Stop tempting me, Jess. I only have so much willpower where you're concerned."

"You do?" For some reason, his confession made her joyously happy.

"Yes," he snapped. "So stop looking so… so kissable."

"What do you want me to do?"

"I don't know. Clamp your lips together. Put mud on your face." He flung his hand through the air. "Anything."

"Okay." She dipped her fingers in the mud by her feet and swiped it across her cheek.

His jaw dropped open. "I was kidding, Jess. Now I need to wipe it…" He lifted his fingers toward her cheek, snatching his hand back before he made contact. His eyes squeezed shut. "I won't look. It'll probably be better this way."

"Maybe you should say what you have to say. Get it over with." She almost proposed a kiss as a good trade for having to listen to him. She wasn't in the mood to be lectured.

"Do you swear never to tell anyone what I'm about to say?"

Though his eyes were still closed, she could read the anxiety on his face. This wasn't going to be a lecture about Parker. Whatever he was going to tell her had him twisted up like a coiled spring.

"I promise." She resisted the urge to hold his hand.

"Okay…" His Adam's apple bobbed in his throat. "Here's why I have to compete in the rodeo."

With his eyes shut, he could almost pretend Jess wasn't sitting beside him, listening to every emotionally wrought word.

Almost.

But her scent, a combination of fresh citrus and mint,

wafted past his nose with the gentle breeze, reminding him of her presence. Yet he didn't fall apart like he thought he would, even when he heard her sniffing beside him. His throat felt tight a few times, and his eyes got watery, but he kept his emotions in check. To her credit, Jess didn't say a word until he was finished.

He felt her soft fingers slide across his hand. He opened his eyes and watched as their fingers interlaced, fitting perfectly together, despite the diminutive size of her hand.

"Cord?"

He looked over as she rubbed the back of her hand across her eyes. The sympathy he saw there had him teetering on the edge. He didn't dare speak, so he nodded, instead.

"Thank you for telling me. I feel like a jerk for prying. I didn't realize it had anything to do with your father."

He looked at her face, still smudged with mud, which did absolutely nothing to make her less attractive. He pulled up the hem of his t-shirt and wiped her face. Her silver eyes gazed up at him through thick lashes. The shirt slipped from his fingers, but his thumb continued to stroke her petal-soft cheek.

As her lips parted, he moved his thumb, brushing across her alluring mouth. When he tilted his head in a silent question, she answered, closing her eyes and pursing her lips to kiss his thumb. Before she could change her mind, he bent his head, and his mouth found hers at last. He was so hungry for her, he wanted to devour her where she sat. But he held himself back, feathering soft kisses on her tender lips. Then he pulled away, just far enough to make her come to him, to show it was her choice.

When her lips found his again, he moved from one corner of her mouth to the other, savoring the soft plumpness of her responsive lips. Then he deepened the kiss, his heart pounding so hard she could've heard it with her own ears. If not, she surely felt it with the fingertips that now rested on his chest. His hand dipped behind her head, tangling in her silky hair. He let his mouth slide from her lips down to her chin and under her jaw, and he buried his nose against her neck, savoring her fresh scent.

As he tore himself away, she opened her eyes halfway, as if her lids were too heavy to lift. Her tongue peeked out to wet her lips, mocking his self-control, which hung by a gossamer thread.

Catching his breath, he spread his lips in a lazy smile, designed to hide the fire that burned in his chest. "Does this mean I can hold your hand in front of Parker?"

She looked everywhere but at him. "No."

That wasn't the answer he wanted.

"I spilled my guts, and you gave me the kiss of a lifetime, but you still won't date me?"

"I shouldn't have kissed you like that." She edged away from him. "Not until Parker's out of the picture."

"I agree. So let me help you get rid of him."

"I'm afraid your idea of doing that might involve a deep lake and cement boots."

He shrugged. "Sounds like a reasonable way to dispose of him."

"You can't kill Parker," she said, rolling her eyes.

Cord stood, offering her a hand up. "I'm not making any promises."

"I'd rather handle him on my own." She let him pull her to her feet.

Her answer stung, but Cord decided not to fight her. If she hadn't made up her mind, he wouldn't push her. He had to show he wasn't a controlling jerk like her ex.

She picked her way back to Shadow's side and mounted the saddle with the ease born from years of practice. "Listen, Cord... I understand why you want to ride in the rodeo, but I can't help being worried. You know you shouldn't compete without the doctor's clearance."

He could've backed out before, but he'd waited too long.

"I'll be fine. My shoulder's barely even sore, now." He climbed into his saddle and followed behind Jess on the trail.

"I know you want to prove yourself," she said. "I have three older brothers, and all of them were in some kind of sport. But sometimes, you have to sit out a game."

"For Pete's sake, my boss is coming all the way from New York to watch me ride a bull. I'm riding. End of discussion."

She took his words literally, clamming up until they reached the open field again. When she finally spoke again, he couldn't see her expression, but her voice shook with emotion.

"Suit yourself, Cord. But if you end up having surgery on that shoulder, don't come crying to me."

Her heels dug into Shadow's flanks, and the horse sped away before he could come up with a suitable clever retort.

Too irritated to follow after her, he turned Blaze back toward home, muttering to himself, "Don't worry. I won't come crying to you… because I don't cry."

12

*J*ess waved her acceptance to the cheering crowd and stepped back through the arena gate.

"Congratulations, Squirt!" A tall, well-muscled man with brown hair held his arms open wide.

She cried out with delight and threw her arms around her brother's neck. "Zander, I didn't know you were coming!"

He picked her up and twirled her around before setting her down on her booted feet. "You were awesome out there. Good to see you back in the saddle."

"Shadow was incredible. He always puts his heart into a race, but he's lost some of his speed. We were lucky we didn't have much competition. That high school girl almost beat me." She gave Zander another hug. "It's so good to see you."

"What am I? Chopped liver?" asked the man beside

him, two inches shorter, with shoulders two inches broader, and a shirt patterned after the Texas flag.

Laughing, she gave him a bear hug, and he returned it, squeezing the breath out of her.

"Thought you were ignoring me." Nick wore a pout, but his green eyes sparkled.

"I shouldn't even be speaking to you." She aimed her best glare his direction. "I know you had Cord spying on me all this time."

"Don't be mad, J.J. Someone has to watch out for you," said Nick.

Jessica dismissed him, addressing Zander. "Did you bring Cohen with you?"

Her oldest two brothers lived in Austin within twenty minutes of each other, and she adored them.

"Cohen's out of town. He might've come if you'd bothered to tell us you were competing." Zander crossed his arms and leaned against the strong metal fence, solid on the bottom and with close horizontal slats on top to protect the audience from injuries. The loud speaker blasted, announcing the next event, the calf roping. Like Nick, Zander wore a straw cowboy hat and seemed oblivious to the appreciative looks from female passersby. "If Nick hadn't called, I wouldn't even be here."

"Sorry, I didn't tell you. But it was no big deal. Just an amateur rodeo." The truth was, she'd been nervous to race after a long hiatus.

"I know you, Squirt. Every competition is a big deal." He wrapped an arm around her shoulder. "We did our part, right? Stayed away so you could concentrate?"

Jess followed the same pattern at every competition—she made her family and friends keep their distance until after she raced.

"That's right. Pre-race hugs are bad luck."

"We saved you a seat with Nanna and Bucky," said Nick. "But I want to talk to Cord before I go back up. Have you seen him around here?"

Just the mention of Cord's name tied her gut into knots. It seemed there was no way Cord *wouldn't* reinjure his right shoulder, holding onto the bull rope. And when that happened, he'd be less able to scramble away from the bull's deadly hooves and horns. Her attempt to talk him out of competing had only made him more determined to do it. She dredged up some anger to cover her real emotion —fear.

"He's probably with all the other bull riders, beating on his chest and making Tarzan calls."

Zander doubled over with laughter. Nick, however, didn't appear to find any humor in her statement.

"Since when do you have something against bull riders?"

"Y'all are too macho for your own good," she retorted. "Otherwise guys like Cord wouldn't be riding with a separated shoulder."

Nick's brows drew together until they almost touched. "Cord told me the doctor cleared him to compete."

His glower grew darker, gathering energy like a storm. She dreaded facing Cord after she sicced her brother on him. But she'd rather Cord be alive, even if he never spoke to her again.

Then Nick's gaze focused on something behind her, surprise widening his eyes. "Parker. What are you doing here?"

With her stomach in her throat, Jess whipped around, her eyes taking in the man who'd dropped her seven months before. Parker Brown stood before her, sporting a western shirt and what must be a brand new cowboy hat. She almost started laughing when she spied cowboy boots sticking out from his creased blue jeans. She had to give him credit for trying hard to impress her. But why the sudden change of heart?

"I came to beg your sister for a second chance."

"Really." Sarcasm filled Nick's single-word response.

Jess couldn't help responding in kind. "Wow, Parker. I've never heard you say something so… *humble*. What happened to you?"

For a fleeting second, she thought she glimpsed anger in his eyes, but then it was gone. He smiled, exposing perfect teeth, which probably cost his parents a fortune. Once, when she complimented his smile, he'd bragged about his Hollywood-style veneers.

"I had a birthday."

His gaze flicked to her brothers, and he pressed his lips tight, refusing to elaborate. But she knew the meaning behind his cryptic statement. He'd turned twenty-four, and inherited his trust fund. He no longer had to please his parents to gain access to money.

Was he pursuing her because he'd truly wanted her all along, and had only ditched her because his parents threatened to cut him off? Or was this his way of demonstrating his rebellion, flaunting her in his parents' faces. Neither scenario seemed particularly desirable.

"We'll leave you two to talk." Zander secured his brother's arm and dragged him away. But he mumbled in Jessica's ear as he passed, "Hope you dump that fancified fart."

Jess chuckled. As her oldest brother, Zander had yet to approve of any of her boyfriends, though he might've disliked Parker the most.

When her brothers were out of sight, Parker moved closer. "I saw you race. Very impressive. It's fascinating how everyone around here is really into this rodeo stuff."

"Kind of like how Dallasites are into charity galas?"

His eye twitched the way it always did when he was getting impatient. "Since your competition's over, do you want to go grab a bite to eat somewhere?"

"If you're hungry, there's plenty to eat, right here. They're selling sausage on a stick and roasted corn-on-the-cob at the food tent."

The crowd cheered as something exciting happened inside the arena. Jess peered through the slats in the fence and saw a calf lying on his side, three of his feet tied, a horse backing up to keep the rope tight, while the competing cowboy waved a hand at the crowd. She couldn't see the time on the board, but judging from the audience response, it must've been fast.

"Okay. We can eat here, then." Parker drew her attention, stretching his mouth into more of a grimace than a smile, as he held his hand out toward her.

She stared at his fingers like they were snakes, unconsciously stuffing her hands in her pants pockets. "You can go eat. I'm heading up to watch the rest of the rodeo."

"You don't want to eat with me?"

"And miss the rodeo?"

What she really didn't want to miss was the possibility of seeing Cord. A quick glance around revealed no sign of him, though she'd hoped he might come by to congratulate her. She told herself he was busy putting out a million fires to keep the rodeo running smoothly. She didn't want to believe the other possibility... that she'd hurt him too badly when she asked him not to compete in the rodeo.

If only she'd kept her big mouth shut. The moment after he'd poured out his heart about riding to please his father was the worst time to criticize his decision, no matter how worried she was. She knew that now. Part of her wanted to search for him and apologize before the competition. But that would go against her own strict rule to avoid distraction during a competition. She certainly didn't want to cause a lapse in concentration during his dangerous ride.

"Are you listening to me?" His voice jerked her attention back.

"Sorry. What did you say?"

Parker's lips tugged down in something akin to a pout. "I drove four-and-a-half hours to get here, and you're not even going to talk to me?"

"Why did you really come? You haven't even called since January."

To her surprise, his eyes got watery, and he looked to the side, his throat convulsing. "My grandfather died."

"Oh, Parker! I'm so sorry!" She'd only met the man once, but he'd been sweet and welcoming—the only one out of Parker's family who seemed to like her. She knew he and Parker had been close.

"You're the only person who understands." He wrapped his arms around her, his voice shaking with barely contained emotion, and she didn't resist.

"He loved you very much. He told me how proud he was of you." She patted Parker's back.

Still clinging to her, he took a shuddery breath. "We hadn't even buried him before everyone was fighting over his money like vultures. All I could think was I don't want to be part of this family anymore."

"I can see where that would make you angry." She wanted to say more, but kept her mouth shut, her heart aching for him.

"That's why you were so good for me. You're different from everyone else I know." He stepped back and quickly wiped his eyes, his gaze aimed toward his shiny new boots. "I guess it was dumb to hope you might take me back."

The crowd cheered again, and Jess glanced wistfully toward the arena, hating that she was missing the action. But it would be an hour or more before the bull riding started, and Parker needed a friend. She could offer him that much.

"Let's go somewhere and talk."

Parker offered his hand again, and this time she didn't have the heart not to take it.

"Thank you," he breathed. "I've been so empty without you."

She saw it then—the handsome guy who'd made her feel so special, like she was one-in-a-million. It was the reason she'd fallen for him. Only after a while, he'd tried to change the very things he'd claimed to admire about her. Had his grandfather's death turned him into a different man?

He started toward the concession tents, tugging on her hand, but she held back.

"You understand we're only talking, right? Friend to friend?"

The emotion that narrowed his eyes seemed more like challenge than acceptance, but he nodded and said, "I understand."

"I'm sorry, sir," Cord told the cowboy, whose lower lip was distended with a dip of tobacco. "But you'll have to wear the protective gear when you ride."

"You see, Jack?" Mason was clearly riled up. "We all have to wear 'em. I don't like it any more than you do."

The man let out an expletive and spit on the ground, leaving a wet, brown stain. "I'm wearing my hat, or I'm not riding."

"Then you'll have to forfeit your entry fee," Cord said. "If anyone rides without a helmet, our insurance policy is invalidated for the whole event. If I let you ride wearing a cowboy hat, and anyone else gets hurt during the rodeo, they'd be out of pocket for their hospital bills. Plus, we could be sued, and we wouldn't be eligible for any events in the future."

"Well that's just stupid," he grumbled. "The professional rodeos don't do that."

"We don't have a pro rodeo budget," Cord explained. "They would've charged us an arm and a leg for a two-day policy, if we hadn't agreed to the helmets."

"Fine. I'll wear it." He spat again, narrowly missing Cord's boot, then stomped away.

"Thanks for talking to him," said Mason. "He wouldn't listen to me."

"Glad I could help. You're already juggling a lot of hats over here, getting the bulls and the riders ready." Likewise, Cord had been putting out one fire after another, running all over the arena, wherever his cell phone beckoned him. Though he hadn't had a minute to rest, he also hadn't had time to get nervous about his upcoming bull ride. "I appreciate you making sure all the i's are dotted and the t's are crossed."

Mason took off his cowboy hat and rubbed his forehead before slapping it back in place. "Speaking of dotting i's, you haven't signed your health affidavit."

"What's it for?"

"Takes the place of a signed health clearance from a physician. States that your doctor cleared you to compete. All you have to do is sign it." Mason dug inside an accordion folder tucked against a wall and retrieved a sheet of paper. He handed Cord the form, along with a pen.

"Do all the competitors sign a form like this?" Cord

tugged at his shirt collar, which was suddenly two sizes too small. "Even if they haven't been injured?"

"If you haven't been injured, you just check box A. But I already checked box B for you and filled out the top. Just need your signature." Mason turned around. "Here. You can use my back to sign it."

Cord laid the paper on Mason's back and set the point of the pen on the signature line. But he couldn't make his hand move.

"What if someone signs this paper, but the doctor hasn't really given them a clean bill of health?"

Mason slowly turned back around, his eyes narrowing. "Are you saying what I think you're saying? Your doctor didn't clear you to ride?"

"I think he's being overly cautious," Cord said, toying with the pen in his hand.

Mason folded his arms over his chest, scowling like an angry school principal. "I thought you just had some bruises and sprains, but nothing was broken."

Cord pointed to his joint. "This shoulder got dislocated. It feels fine now, but I couldn't get the doctor to believe me."

"You said you strained it. You never said a word about dislocating the joint." Mason mumbled something under his breath as he snatched the page from Cord's fingers. "You're not riding tonight."

"Wait a minute." Cord grabbed for the paper, but Mason ripped it to pieces before his eyes.

"Don't be an idiot, Cord."

"You may not believe this, but I'm as tough as any guy

out here." Cord jutted his jaw forward. "All I have is a separated shoulder. You told me you'd even ridden with broken bones before."

"That's true." Mason gestured wildly like he was conducting an orchestra. "But I was nineteen and thought I was invincible. I wasn't. I found out the hard way. You're my age, Cord. You should know better."

"Are you telling me you wouldn't ride tonight if you'd dislocated your shoulder four weeks ago?"

The toe of Mason's boot tapped an impatient rhythm on the dirt. "Last time I dislocated my shoulder, I was out the rest of the season. Missed ten rodeos."

As his words sunk in, Cord felt about an inch tall. As embarrassed as he was to be called out by Mason, he was even more mortified that his boss had flow from New York, just to watch him ride. "I guess I'll get out of your hair, then."

"Not so fast." Mason caught his arm. "If you're as tough as you say you are, you can be my fence-sitter."

"What's a fence-sitter?"

"You sit on the arena fence during the bull rides. If those two young bullfighters get in trouble, you jump down and help them."

Cord's heart thumped so hard and fast, he could hear it inside his head. "Don't I need a doctor's clearance to be a fence-sitter?"

He sincerely hoped so. During his weekend bull riding course, his practice attempt at bullfighting had been terrifying. His teacher had laughingly commended him for drawing the bull away from the rider by running a hundred-yard-dash in a fifty-yard-dash time. He then attempted to convince Cord that his courage would rise to the occasion if he were actually saving a bull rider from a bull instead of merely enticing a bull to chase him. Cord's current panic attack said otherwise.

"You don't need a doctor's clearance, because it's not an official job. But those guys are pretty green, and I prefer to have backup. You won't be alone, most of the time. I'll be up there with you as much as I can be," said Mason. "Don't worry. Your only injury is likely to be the fence making your butt sore."

Mason's laughter was drowned out by the crowd, as the next event was announced... barrel racing. Cord didn't have time to make it up to the grandstands.

"Afraid you're going to miss your girlfriend's race?" Mason gave a knowing smile. Cord was about to protest when Mason pointed to his left. "Go into the empty bucking chute and watch through the gate. I'll join you in a second."

Still feeling a little miffed that Jess hadn't trusted him to ride a bull without getting hurt again, despite the fact he was now excluded from the competition, Cord was surprised to find his fingers shaking as he waited for her race. When he saw her behind the starting gate, the fourth to compete, his heart rate skyrocketed and beads of sweat broke out on his forehead. His hands gripped the metal so tightly, his knuckles blanched. As she rode, her body moving in fluid coordination with Shadow's as if the two were one, a huge sense of pride welled in his chest. She posted a 14.5-second time, the best by a 2-second margin.

Cord cheered and whistled, desperately wishing she could hear his voice over the crowd. As it was, she had no idea he was rooting for her. Mason arrived at his side just as she finished, but let out a celebratory whoop.

The minutes passed like hours as he waited for all the competitors to finish round one and became increasingly agitated, not even comprehending Mason's endless chatter. Then it happened. One of the mares slipped and went down sideways, trapping her rider's leg beneath her. The crowd let out a collective gasp, but soon the girl was on her feet and back on her horse, waving at the crowd.

Nevertheless, Cord had an insane urge to find Jessica and beg her to skip the second round. She could be pinned under Shadow in a fall or thrown off and crushed by the gelding's hooves. Anything could happen. When Jess finally raced again, he could barely watch, anxiety making him hold his breath until her run was over.

Had she been feeling the same way when she asked him not to compete in the bull riding? Cord had been certain her request was motivated by her lack of faith in his abilities. But if she'd felt anything remotely close to his nervous panic, he owed her a huge apology.

When the announcer called her name as the barrel racing champion, she returned to the arena on foot, waving her hat at the crowd. Cord jumped up and down, pumping his fist in the air as if he'd been the actual winner. Watching beside him, Mason McCaffrey regarded him like he'd lost his mind. Secretly, Cord agreed with him.

Mason made a tsking noise as his head moved in a slow shake. "Man, you are *gone* for Jessica, aren't you?"

"I wouldn't say I'm *gone* for her. I like her and all, but—"

Mason rolled his eyes. "Don't deny it. I know a lovesick puppy when I see one."

"But—"

"I'd better get an invitation." Mason's hand slapped Cord's back.

"Invitation?"

"To the wedding!"

Mason doubled over, cackling with laughter. Cord felt heat creeping up his neck, but he gave a good-natured chuckle at McCaffrey's joke.

"We're not that serious," Cord said.

But was he kidding himself?

Hadn't he already begun to order his life around hers? Knowing Jess preferred city life, he'd almost talked himself into leaving Sage Valley. He and Finn had even discussed the possibility of working from Houston, where one of the other partners had an office.

"If you aren't serious, then you won't mind if I dance with her tomorrow night, right?" Mason asked.

"I thought you were taking Ellen to the dance."

"We broke up," Mason said cheerfully. "So I'm glad to hear you and Jessica aren't exclusive."

"We *are* exclusive," Cord was quick to clarify.

"But y'all aren't serious, so a dance or two would be no big deal." Mason rubbed his hands together briskly, like he was warming them by a fire, despite the fact it had only cooled off to about eighty degrees that evening. "This is great news. I thought I'd be sitting on the sidelines all night."

"She won't be dancing with anyone but me," said Cord, his jaw clamping shut like a loggerhead turtle.

Mason laughed, slapping his knees. "Like I said, you are one lovesick puppy."

The only sound Cord could make was a growl.

"I was kidding you, man. I'm going with Ellen. And I promise I won't ask Jess to dance, as long as you guarantee I'm on the guest list."

So irritated he couldn't think straight, Cord forced a laugh, pretending Mason's teasing didn't faze him. Then he gasped as he remembered a tiny detail he'd pushed to the back of his mind.

Parker's here.

Turning on his heel, he dashed out, ignoring Mason's calls. He raced behind the newly added bleachers past the corrals and chutes for the horse events. He'd just seen her come through the outer arena gate a few minutes earlier when her name was announced as the winner. Hopefully, she hadn't gone far.

"Why did every person here pick now to come down and go to the bathroom?" he complained to himself, as he weaved through the people lined up at the porta potties. When he almost ran into a woman with a baby strapped to her, he decided to slow his pace. From the arena he heard the crowd cheering for the first contestant in the calf roping.

As he drew closer to the exit gate, he scanned the crowd, but saw no sign of her. What would he say if he found her? That she looked adorable in her sequin-adorned western shirt? That he was proud of her for winning the barrel racing? That he hoped she could forgive him for getting angry?

That I can't live without her and don't want to try.

He jolted to a stop, as the thought settled in his mind. Was it true?

Someone bumped against him where he stood like a boulder in the middle of a highway.

"Sorry," the stranger said, and Cord repeated the word, barely registering the collision.

Was he really in love with Jessica? Should he tell her? An *I-love-you* would probably send her running for the hills. Yet deep inside, he knew if he didn't tell her, he'd regret it for the rest of his life.

He started walking again, the end of the grandstands in sight. Then he spotted her, and his heart jumped out of his chest. Her shiny brown hair flowed out of her ponytail like a waterfall. His hands twitched, remembering how silky that hair felt between his fingers.

Her luscious lips moved, as if deliberately enticing him. She was talking to someone. A man. Cord's chest constricted, forcing all the air from his lungs. It had to be him—Parker Brown—Jessica's controlling ex-fiancé.

Cord watched in horror as the man wrapped his arms around Jess. She didn't resist. The two clung to each other in passion, like they weren't surrounded by dozens of curious onlookers. When the torturous embrace finally ended, Parker held out his hand.

Don't take it!

After a moment's indecision, her hand slipped into his, and Cord's heart splintered. He grasped at a nearby support pole and leaned against it, squeezing his eyes shut, as if he could unsee what had just happened.

A painful grip on his arm jerked him back to reality. "I've been looking for you, Dennison."

Cord lifted lifeless eyes to face a pair of furious ones. "Hi, Nick," he answered, in a defeated voice.

"Are you crazy?" Nick yelled, attracting the attention of several passersby. "You can't ride with a separated shoulder."

"I know," Cord replied. "I'm not."

"You better listen to... What? You're not riding tonight?"

"No." Cord turned, walking aimlessly the way he'd come.

"Wait. What's wrong with you?" Nick's hand grasped his elbow. "Are you this upset because you can't compete tonight?"

Cord attempted to swallow, with something the size of Africa stuck in his throat. Nick might as well know the truth. "I lost Jess."

Nick chuckled. "Don't worry, buddy. You don't have to keep track of her tonight. I know you're busy running this whole show. But thanks for keeping her safe from all the other dudes this summer."

"I lost her to Parker."

"I know Parker's here." Nick's brows bent together. "But I don't think she'll take him back."

"She already did," Cord said, his voice hoarse. "She hugged him. They walked away holding hands."

Nick's chin protruded. "I won't let it happen."

"Don't you get it? Your sister is smart and independent. She'll do whatever she wants. You can't stop her, and neither can anyone else." Cord tried to take a deep breath, but someone had strapped an iron belt around his chest. "And I didn't even get a chance to tell her."

"Tell her what?"

From Nick's thunderous expression, Cord suspected he already knew the answer. Dating his sister would be a crime worthy of the death penalty in Nick's eyes, but right now, Cord didn't care. At least it would put him out of his misery.

"That I'm in love with her."

13

---

*B*y some miracle, thirty minutes later, Cord was still alive.

"Some watchdog you are," Nick complained. "You were supposed to fend the rabid guys off, not become one of them."

"What can I say? She stuck me in the friend zone, and I tried to claw my way out." From his seat on the pickup tailgate, Cord swung his legs to get his blood circulating again. He'd followed Nick to the parking lot so he could retrieve his cell phone from his truck. "She never led me on, but I couldn't help falling for her. So say whatever you want to me, because nothing's going to make me feel any worse than I already do."

Beside him, Nick made a sound that could've been a laugh or a groan. "I guess there could be worse things than having you as a brother-in-law."

"Have you listened to anything I said?" Irritation rose to the surface, and he relished feeling something other than dead. "She doesn't love me. I thought there was hope if I stuck with it, but she made her choice… Parker."

"I have a great idea how to get rid of that dude," said Nick. "Let's sign him up for the bull riding competition. I'd love to watch him get bucked to the ground in his fancy new western duds."

"Bull riding!" Cord leapt off the tailgate, scanning his phone for the time. "I have to get back before it starts!"

"I thought you weren't competing." Nick eyed him with suspicion before standing up to slam the tailgate closed.

"I promised McCaffrey I'd be on standby in case the bullfighters need backup." They started back toward the arena at a brisk pace.

"Why you? You've got to be greener than the bullfighters you're paying to do the job."

Cord's already-shaky confidence took a nose-dive. "Probably punishment. Sitting on a fence for a couple of hours in retribution for trying to compete without a doctor's release."

"That seems fair." Nick chuckled as he glanced at his cell phone. "I doubt J.J.'s even got her phone with her. She hasn't sent any messages. But she'll probably come sit with us—she and Parker, I guess. What do you want me to say to her?"

"She was worried, so let her know I'm not riding tonight. But please don't tell her what I told. I'm humiliated enough."

"You don't want me to put in a good word for you?" Nick grinned, his eyes crinkling in the corners.

"Best I can tell, Jess does the opposite of whatever you

suggest. So, please don't." Cord sighed. "Although it's too late to matter, anyway, now that she's back with Parker."

"I think you're overestimating Parker. Or underestimating J.J. He was a jerk to her. I can't believe she'd take him back."

"You didn't see them together," said Cord.

Surprisingly, Nick didn't answer with a smart retort, though he scowled like he was thinking one.

"I have to tell Mr. Anderson I'm not riding." Cord jotted off an apologetic text to Finn, who was up in the stands somewhere. "He flew all the way from New York to watch me ride."

"Wow! Will you introduce us after the rodeo?"

"Sure." Cord couldn't match his friend's enthusiasm. "This is so humiliating."

"Look at it this way..." Nick's laughter bubbled out as he clapped Cord on the back. "It's probably not as humiliating as your bull ride would've been."

At first, Jessica felt sorry for Parker. No doubt he was devastated about his grandfather. But by the time they had talked and eaten their fill of corn dogs and turkey legs, he was beginning to push the boundaries. Twice, he'd put his arm around her shoulder, and she'd firmly removed it. In the grandstands he'd sat with his leg plastered against hers, closing any distance she attempted to make between them. It was particularly awkward with her grandparents sitting behind them. She'd whispered to Nanna about Parker losing his grandfather, but Nanna's sympathetic expression only lasted a fleeting second.

Nick was no help at all, making even more snide remarks than usual, from his seat next to Nanna. "Nice boots, Parker. Did you order those from *Cowboys R Us*?"

"At least my boots don't smell like cow manure," Parker retorted, with a congenial smile.

"That's enough, Nick." Jess raised her eyebrows in warning before her brother could respond with one of his off-color jokes about cow manure. "Watch what you say in front of Nanna."

"Don't mind me," said Nanna, with a mischievous grin.

As the announcer proclaimed the beginning of the bull riding event, Jessica's stomach twisted into a pretzel. She wiped her palms on her jeans, the sweat having nothing to do with the temperature. She just knew something terrible was going to happen to Cord, and the last words between them had been cross ones. She'd hoped Nick might be able to talk him out of competing, but as far as she knew, that didn't happen. If only she could find a way to ask her brother about Cord without alerting Parker.

She looked over her shoulder. "Hey Nick, did you ever find your friend?"

"What friend?" Nick batted his long lashes, like he didn't know who she meant.

"Cord," she rasped.

"Cord?" He took off his hat and scratched his head. "Oh! You mean Cord Dennison? Yep. I found him."

"Well?" she growled, as the first bull sprang from the chute amid audience cheers. "What did he say?"

"About what?" Nick cocked his head.

"You know what I'm asking. Did you talk him out of competing tonight?"

"As a matter of fact, no." His stare was so intense, she looked away.

"Oh."

The crowd cheered and clapped, though the cowboy got bucked off well before the eight-second mark.

"I'm surprised you care what Cord does," said Nick, squinting his eyes at something.

She followed the line of his gaze and noticed Parker's hand on her knee. How long had that been there?

With a side swipe, she knocked the offending hand away. "For goodness sake, Parker. Keep your hands to yourself."

"But baby, I thought—"

"Be quiet. I'm talking to Nick." She turned to glare at her brother, who looked even more smug than usual. What had he meant with that subtle jab about Cord? "What did Cord tell you?"

"Cord told me a lot of things." Nick crossed his arms, his gaze on the arena below, where the bull circled around and finally trotted back toward the open gate.

"Like what?" Jessica's patience was wearing thin, and Nick seemed to be enjoying it.

He leaned forward and lowered his voice, though it was still loud enough that their neighbors could hear. "He might've mentioned seeing you and Parker hugging and holding hands."

She sucked in air so fast she choked.

"I guess your secret's out," Nick said sarcastically. "Everyone knows you two are back together, now."

"I'm glad everyone knows," said Parker, his lips stretched in an arrogant smile.

"There's nothing to know," Jess said. "We are *not* back together. Didn't you explain that to Cord?"

"I would've explained everything to Cord," Nick said with a shrug, "if only my baby sister had explained it to me. But evidently, she's been keeping a lot of secrets. So, my hands were tied." He demonstrated, stretching his wrists out together.

"Do you even wonder why I don't tell you things?"

Her eyes stung as she fought to hold onto her frayed emotions. Everything was going wrong. The crowd exclaimed as one, rising to their feet. What had happened? Was it Cord? Was he hurt? She stood up, craning to see between the people in front of her. A rider was down, but one bullfighter quickly lured the bucking bull away while the other helped the rider to his feet and out of harm's way, as it happened 90% of the time. But she couldn't shake the sick feeling in her gut, that something bad was going to happen on Cord's ride.

Jess sank to her seat, dropping her face into her hands. She felt a gentle touch on her shoulder, then heard a whisper. "Sorry, J.J." Nick's hand tightened. "I was only teasing you. Cord's not riding tonight."

Jess whipped around so fast her neck hurt. "Do you mean it? Cord's not getting on a bull?"

"He's not competing." Nick had the good grace not to

smirk. "But I wasn't kidding about the other part. He really does think you're back with Parker."

Her stomach did a double flip. She had to see Cord. To set him straight about Parker. To apologize for hurting his feelings. To tell him the truth about how she felt. But how did she really feel?

The truth was that winning the barrel race was like an empty victory without Cord there to share it. She didn't want to be friends with Cord anymore. She wanted to be more than friends. A lot more.

"Wait a minute…" Jess tugged on Nick's shirt to pull his attention away from the arena, where the buzzer had sounded, indicating the rider had made the eight-second mark. "You're not upset? About me and Cord?"

"Who's Cord?" asked a grumpy-looking Parker.

"None of your business," said Nick and Jess in unison.

"I wasn't thrilled at first, but the idea's growing on me." He looked pointedly at Parker. "It could be worse."

Jess grinned at her brother and stood up. "Where is he?"

"He's hanging around at the bull chutes in case there's an emergency."

She was already bounding down the stairs when Nick yelled, "They may stop you if you try to go back there."

Without a pause, she shouted back, "They can try!"

CORD'S ADRENALINE surged as Mason settled onto the back

of the bull, who did his best to buck him off while still inside the chute.

"Save it for the show, Dynamite," Mason mumbled, jamming his right hand under the bull rope.

Mason seemed thrilled to draw Dynamite Mojo for his ride. The 1800-pound bull had a reputation for being really tough to ride, but that meant a better score... *if* the rider could stay on for the full eight seconds. In bull riding competitions, both the rider and the bull were given performance scores, up to fifty points each, so a perfect ride would score 100.

As Cord had watched the first four riders, he'd gradually become more appreciative that he'd been disqualified from the competition. Neither of the practice bulls at his weekend school had been as challenging as the gentlest of the bulls at the rodeo.

During two of four rides, Mason had sat atop the fence with Cord, watching the competition. Mason had jokingly nicknamed the bullfighters *Red* and *Green*. "They're both pretty green," Mason explained, "but Sam has red hair."

Thankfully, Red and Green had done their jobs, and Cord hadn't had to leave his perch.

But the night's not over, his jittery brain reminded him.

Dynamite surged against the gate, the clang of metal making Cord jump out of his skin. But Mason calmly lifted his left hand in the air. He nodded his head, and the gate burst open.

Dynamite erupted from the gate straight into a series of bucking rotations, spinning in a circle so fast that Cord got dizzy watching. Abruptly, the bull shifted the other direction. Then he jumped in the air, twisting his body, and spreading his legs in the air. Cord held his breath, certain Mason was about to fall, but the cowboy stuck to the bull like Velcro. Dynamite started clockwise rotations again, but Mason stayed centered, his left hand high in the air, his feet kicking forward and back, in rhythm with the bucking bull. Seemingly more furious that Mason was still clinging to his back, Dynamite rocked forward and kicked his rear legs so high that Mason had to lean back to stay on, his body almost vertical.

Then the buzzer sounded! Mason had made the eight seconds. He had only to jump off to his right and escape the bull's fury.

But before Mason could dismount, Dynamite rocked up on his back feet and reared his head, impacting Mason's helmet. Then the bull kicked his rear feet high in the air, and Mason went forward on his belly, his feet flying above the bull's haunches. When his legs came down, he was off the bull... on the wrong side.

He's hung up!

"Get the tail," Cord yelled at the bullfighters, though they surely didn't need his advice. Meanwhile, Dynamite continued to buck and twist in a circle, giving the young men no chance to dart in and grab the rope from his right side. Dazed and stumbling, Mason could barely keep his footing enough to avoid the bull's hooves and horns, much less jump on top and free his hand.

Before Cord realized what he was doing, he was off the fence, running toward the bull. Red leapt in front of Dyna-mite, waving his hands in an effort to get the bull's attention and stop the mad rotations, while Green tried to maneuver where he could grab the tail of the rope and free Mason's hand.

Just as Cord got close, the bull reversed his rotations, and Mason stumbled, hanging by his tethered hand, his legs sliding under the bull. For a split second, Cord saw an opening. He dashed behind the bull's thrashing horns and grabbed Mason under his arms, hoisting him up. By some miracle, Green got through and flung himself at the bull from the other side, leaping up to yank the rope tail, which released Mason's hand from the twisted bull rope.

His arm fell free.

Supporting most of his friend's weight, Cord backed away from Dynamite, watching his every move. In the back of his mind he heard Manuel Lopez drilling rule number one into his head, "Never take your eyes off the bull."

Meanwhile Red and Green did their best to chase or lure the bull out of the arena. But Dynamite balked at the gate and turned, barreling straight for Cord and Mason, with Red and Green chasing behind him. Cord let Mason slide to the ground and jogged to the side, waving his hands to attract the bull. Ignoring his efforts, the bull aimed toward Mason, who now lay helpless on the ground. Cord had no choice. He screamed at the top of his lungs and flapped his arms as he ran directly toward the charging bull…

No one stopped Jess when she weaved her way between

the bull pens toward the chutes. She spotted Cord, balanced on top of the horizontal-slatted fence, intent on the bull rider who had the audience cheering with excitement. Now that she was here, how was she going to do this? A private conversation would be impossible, unless he was willing to abandon his post.

Or… I could just climb up and sit on the fence with him.

A roar went up from the grandstands, providing the perfect cover for her to sneak up on him. As she tiptoed closer, she grinned, imagining his surprise when she appeared beside him. He would be so shocked he might forget all about being upset with her.

I might even get up the courage to use the L-word.

Just as her hand touched the fence, she felt a movement, and Cord jumped off into the arena.

Something must've happened!

Jess darted around the corner into the bucking chute, alongside two other cowboys who were watching through the gate with horror-stricken faces. With both hands gripping the metal, she saw the scene unfold. Cord was up against the bull's shoulder, supporting the bull rider who appeared to be tangled in the rope.

"Yes!" yelled the cowboy beside her, when Cord dragged the injured rider away from the furious bull.

The crisis appeared to be over, with the bullfighters urging the bull toward the exit. One second, he was trotting toward the open gate. The next, he balked and turned, charging directly at Cord and the bull rider.

Run, Cord! What are you doing? Don't run toward the bull!

The bull hooked Cord with his horns, tossing him into

the air like a rag doll. When he landed on the ground in a heap, he didn't move.

The crowd went silent, except for a single extended scream of terror. Several seconds passed before Jess realized the eerie sound was coming from her own throat.

14

*C*ord blinked, struggling to open his eyes. Lying on his back, he saw the evening sky and arena lights above him and a fence against his left shoulder. Voices swirled around him, echoing like a crowd in a shopping mall. The sound faded as pain pushed its way in, eclipsing everything else in his brain.

"Oh. You're awake." A female face appeared above him, blond hair pulled back in a bun. "Can you tell me where you hurt?"

"Everywhere. Especially right here." Cord touched his ribs on his right side and realized someone had opened his shirt. "It's worse when I breathe."

"I recommend doing it anyway," she said, with a straight face. "The alternative isn't great."

"I'll keep that in mind." He'd just have to take tiny breaths so his ribs didn't move. He took in his surroundings. He was lying on the ground in one of the arena corrals, a fence next to him.

"What's your name?" A pen light appeared in the woman's hand, shining in his eyes.

"Cord. What's yours?"

"I'm Mandy Jackson, paramedic. Can you tell me what day it is?"

"Uhmm…" He searched his memory, but came up with nothing.

"How about the month? Or the year?"

"I can't think…"

"What's the president's name?"

He wracked his brain, but came up with nothing. "Why do you need to know who the president is?"

"It's a test."

Cord considered her problem. "Why don't you Google it?"

Though it seemed like a perfectly reasonable suggestion, Mandy responded with an irritated growl. "Can you tell me what happened to you?"

"I don't know…" Fuzzy pictures passed through his mind. Someone riding a bull. Falling off. "Mason! Is Mason okay?"

"I'm right here, man. All good."

Mason's voice came from somewhere past Cord's feet. But when Cord tried to push up on his elbows to see him, someone jabbed a white-hot sword all the way through his chest and out the back. At least, that's what it felt like.

"Oww!" Cord groaned. "That hurts like the dickens!"

"That's what happens when you play with a bull's horns," said Mason.

"Hey, Jack." Mandy spoke into her cell phone. "We're

coming in from the rodeo with two injured. Patient one with compound fracture of tibia and fibula and class one concussion. Patient two with blunt trauma to the chest, unknown associated injuries, and class two concussion."

"Mason, you broke your leg?" Determined to get his head off the ground, Cord struggled to a sitting position, ignoring the nauseating pain, and leaned his back against the fence. He lifted a weak hand toward the curious onlookers who were peering through the opposite fence, twenty feet away.

"It's broken, alright. You can see the bone. It sucks, but it could've been worse. Thanks to you, it wasn't."

Cord glanced at Mason's leg, glad a bandage covered any exposed bone. "My mind is foggy. I don't remember doing anything."

"After my leg snapped, you kept me on my feet and dragged me out of there. At least until Dynamite got his horns on you. Aren't you glad I made you put that vest on?"

Cord looked down at his bare chest, which was swollen and abraded, but not bleeding. "Yeah, I'm not fond of the idea of having extra holes in my body." He fumbled in a vain attempt to button his shirt. "Awww, man! They ripped my buttons off."

"Yeah. They cut my jeans to get to this leg."

Cord tried to fasten his thick protective vest across his tender skin, but gave up and left it gaping.

"Sorry your leg got broken."

"That's what happens when you stick it under an 1800-pound bull. Worth it, though. I scored an eighty-six!"

Mason seemed awfully cheery for a man with a compound fracture.

"Congratulations. But doesn't it hurt?"

"Pain meds are kicking in. Kind of floating, right now."

"I need some of those for these ribs. I think they may be broken, this time."

"Naaah, you're tough. You don't need pain meds." Mason's words slurred. "You'll make a good bull rider someday."

"Don't think so. I'm done with bull riding, forever."

"That's good to know," said a familiar voice. "I need you to stay alive long enough to finish our project."

Cord ducked his chin. "Hello, Finn."

Except for the times they'd both been in the company gym, he'd never seen his boss so casually attired. Though Phantom Enterprises was famous, few would recognize one of the owners wearing jeans, and a t-shirt that read, "Gamer. Real life is just a hobby."

"Your chest looks horrible." Finn's brows knotted. "Not that I'm surprised. When that bull flung you into the air, I thought you were dead."

"If it weren't for this vest, I probably would be." Cord tried to shift positions, his efforts sending a slice of pain through his chest. He sucked in a hissing breath.

"I'll sit down so it's easier to talk." To Cord's horror, his boss plopped onto the dirt beside him and leaned against the fence. "That woman at the gate almost wouldn't let me in here. She was totally immune to my charms."

His grin indicated he found the situation amusing, rather than frustrating.

"Yeah, she seemed irritated that I got injured." Cord picked at a thread where a button was missing from his shirt. "I'm sorry you came out here for nothing."

"The trip was productive. I had a meeting in Houston with Cole before I drove over here," Finn said. "But I wouldn't have missed watching you get gored by a bull and somehow live to tell about it. I'm waiting for you to walk on water."

Two paramedics walked past with a litter and set it on the ground beside Mason.

"Finn, I hate to tell you this, but I think I'll be staying here in Sage Valley after all."

"I thought you wanted to work from the Houston office?"

"Things have changed…"

Finn heaved an audible sigh. "By any chance, does this have something to do with a woman?"

Heat rose up from his neck to his hairline. "There *was* a woman, but not anymore. She was the reason I was interested in Houston." Cord fidgeted with the zipper on his vest. "You probably think it's dumb to make career decisions based on a girl."

"It depends," Finn said. "Do you love her?"

"I do. But she doesn't. She got back with her ex-fiancé tonight."

Finn twisted, aiming his scrutinizing gaze at Cord. "If you love her, nothing is more important. Not your job. Not your location. And especially not your pride."

Cord finally understood the term *dumbstruck*. He was so shocked to hear Finn's advice, he couldn't respond.

"Have you told her?" Finn asked.

"Uh… not exactly."

"That would be a *no*. What are you waiting for?"

"Just a minute. Aren't you the guy who swore he was never getting married? Seems like you're giving the opposite advice to me."

Finn sagged against the fence, staring ahead. "Cord, you probably don't realize this, but I have cystic fibrosis."

"What does that mean?" he asked, though he was afraid to hear the answer.

"It means the life expectancy for someone like me is only thirty-seven years." Finn climbed to his feet and dusted off his jeans. "But if I were healthy, like you, I wouldn't let anything stand between me and the woman I love."

"Oh." He wanted to say something more, but what could he say? Should he rant about how unfair life is? Should he offer a trite everything-works-out-for-the-best?

"I'd better go. They've got the ambulance pulled up to the gate. And the dragon-lady is giving me the evil-eye," said Finn, his eyes crinkling in the corners. "Let me know what they find at the hospital."

"About my job. I guess I'll—"

"Don't worry. Whatever happens, we'll work something out." Finn waved as he strolled away, stopping to speak to Mandy.

"Looks like my ambulance is ready," called Mason as he passed by on his litter. "I'll see you at the hospital."

Cord shivered at the thought. His memories of the hospital were of his dad hooked up to wires and tubes like a science experiment. "I don't like hospitals," he mumbled under his breath.

"Cord Dennison!" a familiar voice called. "You'd better be dead. Because if you're not, I'm going to kill you."

Nick's joke had Cord smiling for the first time since he woke up.

"Maybe you should wait to see whether I'm dead or not before you tease me about it."

"I'd know if you were dead. This is Sage Valley." Nick loomed over him with a jovial expression. "There's no *patient privacy* here. Half the people here are watching through the fence, and the other half are listening to the PA system broadcast your health updates to the rodeo grounds and three surrounding counties."

The laugh Cord couldn't suppress wracked his body with stabs of pain. "Ow! You really are killing me."

"It's payback for screwing up my sister." Nick sat beside him, propped against the fence. "She's on a bench by the spiced pecan stand, crying her eyes out, and I can't get her to come in here and talk to you."

"What's wrong with her?" Had Parker upset her? Cord would chase the man down and pommel him into the ground... if only someone would help him stand up.

"She's a woman," Nick said, as if that explained everything. "She said something about your injury being all her fault and how you must hate her now." He scrunched his shoulders, sheepishly. "Could be because I told her you saw her with Parker."

The puzzle pieces fell into place—Jess felt guilty about her choice.

If I coerce her into choosing me over Parker, I'm no better than him.

"Tell her I respect her decision," Cord said, trying to convince himself, as well as Nick. "Tell her if Parker's who she really wants, I'm happy for her."

Speaking the words out loud made him want to throw up.

"Are you *sure* that's what you want me to say?" Nick flashed a twisted grin.

"Not when you're wearing a smirk the size of your ego," Cord said. "What am I missing?"

"Maybe one tiny little detail." Nick's eyebrows danced on his forehead. "J.J. gave Parker the boot."

Cord's breath caught in his throat, hope springing to life again. If Nick was right, Cord still had a chance with Jess. He'd have to be patient and stay in the friend-zone, but eventually, she might learn to love him. As long as he didn't push her.

"I need to talk to her," said Cord, as he tried to get to his feet. "Help me up."

"What are you doing? You can't just walk out of here." Nick stood, grasping Cord's arm.

"Why not?"

"You have to go to the hospital to get checked out."

"To get poked and prodded and told I have broken ribs and there's nothing they can do? I don't think so."

Nick jerked his head toward the front of the corral where the paramedics were loading Mason into the ambulance. "You won't be able to get past that blond bulldog at the gate."

"I will if you change shirts with me and let me borrow your hat." Cord took his vest off and tossed it against the fence. "Quick, while they're busy with Mason."

With a rueful shake of his head, Nick unfastened his buttons and slipped his shirt off. "If I get carted away to the hospital in your place, you'd better come rescue me."

"Don't worry." Cord winced as he contorted to slide into Nick's slightly-too-large Texas shirt. "The worst they'll probably do at the hospital is stick you with a big-dog needle and give you an enema."

Nick snorted. "They'd have to catch me, first. Hey… where're your buttons?" He stretched the sides of the shirt together. "Never mind. It doesn't reach anyway."

Cord snatched the cowboy hat from Nick's head and slapped it on, pulling it low over his eyes. "She's at the pecan-stand, right?"

Nick nodded, taking Cord's spot against the fence. "Good luck with the bulldog."

"I'll get past her." With his chin tucked down, Cord took a few trial steps, trying not to wince.

"I was talking about J.J." Nick roared with laughter.

FOR THE THIRD TIME, Jessica wiped her face with her fingers and took a deep breath, working up her courage.

I have to go see Cord. What's the worst that can happen? He already hates me, so it can't get any worse.

Nothing but her stubborn pride was standing in her way. She didn't want to face him now and admit what she should've known weeks ago. She was in love with him. Why couldn't she have seen it before she hurt his feelings?

She edged forward to rise from the bench, but her legs refused to cooperate. With her face in her hands, she leaned forward, her hair cascading down like a blanket.

A man stopped in front of her, wearing jeans and cowboy boots, too dirty to recognize. With a quick glance, she spied Nick's t-shirt, and her spirit sank. That her brother was already back from seeing Cord wasn't a good sign. The conversation must not have gone well, or Nick would be cracking one of his usual jokes.

Closing her eyes, she slumped against the back of the bench in defeat.

"Is this seat taken?"

"Cord?" She looked up, her heart beating inside her throat. "What are you doing here? And why are you wearing Nick's shirt?"

His smile looked strained, but it still made her insides turn to Jell-O. Or maybe ice cream… melted.

"I'm hiding from a beautiful blonde named Mandy."

"Who's she? An old girlfriend?" A bit of jealousy crept into her voice, though she knew she didn't have the right to it.

"Mandy's a paramedic who's bound to have figured out Nick and I switched shirts by now. She's evil. She's trying to make me go the hospital."

"Don't you need to go?"

"No. I'm fine." He flashed his knee-weakening dimples. Lucky she was sitting down. "I'd rather take a walk with you."

She took the hand he offered, but noticed he winced when he helped her stand up. "Cord, you lied to me. You're hurt!"

"I promise to go to the hospital later. I'll even let you drive me. But don't you think we need to talk?"

She looked down to their joined hands and whispered, "Yes."

Fingers laced together, he led her away from the bright lights of the arena, down the path that wound around toward the river, with the moon lighting their way. His gait was definitely slower than usual, though steady, and she worried that he was hiding how badly he was injured.

As the noise of the crowd faded, only the chirps of crickets and frogs rang in their ears. He was quiet, probably waiting for her to apologize. For once, she was ready to swallow her pride.

"I'm sorry, Cord. I'm sorry for everything."

"Everything?"

His solemn expression tore at her heart. She must've hurt his feelings even worse than she realized.

"Everything. For what I said this morning. For letting Parker come. For not being honest."

"Will you tell me the truth?" His voice shook with emotion. "Are you still in love with Parker?"

"No." Her answer was quick and firm, but he didn't respond. What was he thinking? At least he was still holding her hand. Surely that was a good sign.

"How do you feel about *me*?" he asked.

With her face burning, she was glad for the cover of darkness. "I like you."

Why did my voice come out weird and raspy? He probably thinks I'm trying to sound seductive.

They walked on in silence, and she got more embarrassed with every step. He hadn't replied, and she knew why. He must not like her anymore. He must be trying to figure out how to let her down easy. After what seemed like an hour—probably more like sixty seconds—she jerked to a stop, ripping her hand from his grasp.

"Why don't you say something? If you can't forgive me, I can take it. Just tell me what you're thinking."

His sigh was deep and heavy. He reached for her hands and lifted them together to press his lips to her fingers. "I don't know what to say. Because tonight, I realized I've been taking my life for granted. So I want to be honest and tell you how I really feel, but I don't know how you'll react."

"Try me," she breathed, listening to him, over the noisy pulse in her ear. "Tell me the truth."

"How about if I show you?"

His hands rose and cupped her face, the fingers of one hand sliding along her jaw to tilt her chin up, leaving a trail of burning lava behind. Even in the moonlight, his eyes sparkled, drawing her into their crystal depths. His mouth lowered to her ear, his warm breath sending tingles down her spine.

"You're so beautiful, Jess. Just looking at you makes my heart ache. I have to touch you to believe you're real."

Tears sprang to her eyes. "Nobody's ever called me beautiful before."

"Then every other guy was either blind or stupid,

because you're incredible. And the amazing thing is you're beautiful on the inside, too."

His lips moved in a scalding line from her ear, along her cheek, to her mouth. When he pressed his lips to hers, it felt as if their souls were singing together. His kiss, tender at first, then hungry, triggered exploding stars under her eyelids. His hand tangled in her hair, pulling her against him as he deepened the kiss. Blood rushed to her head, and the world tilted. She clung to him against the dizzying flood of sensations, her arms wrapped around his back.

He let out a moan. "Ow… my ribs…"

"I'm so sorry!" She pulled away. "I forgot you were injured."

"I don't care about the pain. It hurts way more to be without you." He reached for her hands and kissed each one, placing them firmly around his neck. "I don't ever want to feel that again. Not ever."

His hands cradled her head as he looked deep into her eyes. "I love you, Jessica."

Her heart thumped against her ribcage, warmth rushing through her veins. "I—"

"Shhh!" He put a finger to her lips. "I know you're not ready to hear it, but I had to tell you. We don't know how many days we have left on this earth. None of us are guaranteed tomorrow. So I don't want to waste a day, pretending I only like you as a friend."

"But I—"

"You bring out the best in me, Jess. You make me want to be a better man. And you aren't afraid to tell me when

I'm being stupid. I may not like hearing it at the time, but I love you for it."

"I'm so—"

"There's no pressure." He waved his hand in front of her face. "I'm willing to wait as long as I have to. That is, if you think there's a chance that someday, in the future, you might feel the same way."

"I—"

"But I'm not pushing you. Do you understand? I'm not like Parker."

"Cord!" His name exploded out of her mouth, as she stomped her foot.

"What?" Wide eyed, he took a step back.

"Stop cutting me off!" Her hands were balled up so tight her fingernails bit into her palms.

"Okay…" He blinked at her.

"I was trying to say I love you, too."

"You do?" The muscles in his throat seemed to convulse. "Because it sounds kind of like you hate me."

"No, I'm just frustrated because you wouldn't let me talk." She folded her arms over her chest. "But, I love you. I really do. I just hadn't figured out how to tell you."

"You really love me? Are you sure?" He pried her tightly twisted arms apart and took her hands, rubbing his thumbs across her fingers in a way that made her irritation float away like smoke in the wind.

"Don't get a big head or anything," she said, "but I've been in love with you since I was thirteen."

His dimples danced. "I'm sorry I didn't notice you back then, but your brother would've killed me. Literally."

"And you would've been arrested."

"That, too."

"It was a crush back then," she said. "But now, it's the real th—"

Cord cut her off again. But this time he did it with a kiss that made her toes curl inside her boots.

And she didn't complain… not one bit.

EPILOGUE

"Good morning, Cord." With her hands in dishwater up to her elbows, Sharon looked over her shoulder. "I'm afraid I just put all the breakfast stuff away, but you're welcome to heat up some leftovers. We had sausage and egg casserole."

"Thanks, Sharon. But I've already eaten." Cord hung his hat on a hook and shut the kitchen door behind him.

"Jess'll be right down. She ran upstairs to brush her teeth."

"We're heading down to the stables for a quick ride." Cord popped a mint in his mouth in anticipation of a private moment.

"Do you have room in your car for Bucky and me tomorrow morning? Neither one of us likes driving in Dallas."

"We're taking Mom's Suburban to Jessica's graduation, so there should be plenty of room."

A noise like a stampede reverberated through the house. Smiling, Cord moved toward the stairs as Jess galloped down and launched into his arms. Lifting her off the ground, he spun in a slow circle, kissing the lips he'd missed so much.

"Three weeks was way too long." Jess gave a blissful sigh when she finally came up for air.

"But you finished your finals, and we never have to do it again." Cord loosened his grip, letting her slide down until her boots touched the floor.

Sharon cleared her throat. "You know, Jessica's parents are coming down for Jessica's graduation. It would be a perfect opportunity for someone to talk to her dad about you-know-what…"

"Nanna!" Jessica's cheeks flushed an adorable shade of pink.

Cord chuckled. He'd already flown up to Oklahoma to formally ask for her parents' blessing. "Thanks, Sharon. I'll keep that in mind."

"Jess, before you go out, Bucky and I have something for you." Sharon dried her hands on a dishtowel and snagged a card from the outside pocket of her purse, passing it to Jess.

She ripped it open, her jaw dropping like she'd seen a ghost. "$500? Nanna, this is too much."

"We can afford it now… all because of Cord."

Much to Cord's embarrassment, the Buchanans had thanked him almost every day for solving the mystery behind the plunge in the ranch's profits. He'd discovered a tax assessment a few years back, categorizing most of the acreage as business property, without an agriculture exemption. The error had cost them tens of thousands. Bucky had always trusted his good friend and CPA to handle those details. But that one had passed away, and the new accountant, only performing general accounting tasks, had never questioned the tax valuation.

"Getting your ag exemption back was only half the battle," said Cord. "I can't take credit for all the expansion you've done. The ranch has never looked better."

"We're just glad your boss is letting you work in Sage Valley. Finn is such a nice young man. We'd love to have him come stay at the ranch." Sharon gave an exaggerated wink. "I assume you'll invite him to the *wedding*."

"You know, Nanna," Jess said, "Cord might decide to go back to New York City just to get away from my meddling grandmother."

"I prefer the term *helpful* over *meddling*." Her mischievous grin showed no remorse.

Cord grabbed Jessica's hand, folding their fingers together. "I had to stay here once Jess said she wanted to teach at Sage Valley High School."

"Hey!" An adorable frown line appeared between her eyes. "I told you I could handle New York, if that's what you wanted."

"But I didn't think New York could handle *you*. And besides…" He tapped the heels of his cowboy boots. "They wouldn't let me wear these with my silk suits."

She grinned up at him, smoky eyes filled with humor. Discovering they both wanted to stay in Sage Valley had been such a relief. After that, nothing stood in the way of them being together. Nothing but her finishing her degree.

Tomorrow was her graduation. He'd waited patiently

for that to happen, but now his patience had worn thin…
very thin… practically nonexistent. He wanted to marry
this woman. The sooner, the better. But he still had to pop
the question. And part of him worried she might find some
reason to turn him down. It was only a tiny part, but it
made his insides twist into a tangled mess.

Jess had planned to enjoy a romantic stroll to the stables,
but Cord was practically dragging her along by the hand.

"What's the rush?"

He flinched and slowed his pace, a rush of red zooming
into his face. "I figured you'd be in a hurry to see Shadow."

"I did miss him a lot."

"More than me?" He blinked his starry eyes in a classic
fishing-for-compliments move.

"Hmm… He *is* handsome. And he listens to me and
never gives away my secrets."

"Shadow's told me a secret or two." Cord's dimples
winked at her.

"Like what?"

He flung the stable doors open and swept his hand to
the interior with a grand gesture. "See for yourself."

Jess took a tentative step inside, spying nothing out of
the ordinary. But as she approached Shadow's stall she
noticed a saddle displayed on the stand outside his door.
Within seconds, she recognized the beautiful tooled leather
and hand stitching.

"You got my saddle! It's the one I've been wanting

forever." She threw her arms around Cord's neck and kissed him, knocking both of their hats to the stable floor. "How did you know?"

"I told you, Shadow tells me all sorts of things." In his stall, Shadow whinnied his agreement, and Cord chuckled. "And I might've gotten a little help from Laurel. I called her to ask what to get you for graduation."

"Thank you so much." She pressed close and hugged him tight, breathing his clean scent. "I can't believe it's only been a year since you strutted into the kitchen and pretended you knew who I was. My whole life, before that day, seems dull and monotone. I call it B.C.—before Cord."

His lips pressed against the top of her head as his hands stroked her back, rippling pleasure up her spine. "When I'm with you, all my senses are more acute. I can see better, hear better, feel better, taste better."

"Can you smell better? Because that's not necessarily a good thing when you're mucking a stall."

His chuckle rumbled in her ear. "Are you sure you like your saddle?"

"I love it," she said, without bothering to look at it again. She'd stared at pictures for hours at a time, so she had every inch of it memorized. "And I love the guy who gave it to me."

"But I want you to check it closely before we use it. I want to make sure it's perfect."

Reluctantly, she pulled away from the warmth of his embrace. "I'm sure it's perfect, but I'll check it over."

Her fingers traced the intricate stitching on the edge of

the seat jockey and fender. Every part of the saddle had a hand-tooled pattern, including the seat and the pommel. Then she noticed the saddle horn. It had a beautiful, engraved cap with her initials. At first, she only noticed the first and last letters, J and P. But then she noticed the middle initial, larger than the other two… an ornate D.

Her breath caught in her throat. She turned around to find Cord on one knee, with a small black velvet box in his outstretched hand. She pressed her hand against her chest, trying to stop her heart from bursting out.

"Jessica Jolene Powell, I love you. More than life. More than anything. I love you so much my chest aches. If you'll let me, I'll spend the rest of my life showing you how much I love you. So, what do you say? Will you marry me and make me the happiest man in the world?"

The rare glistening of his sapphire eyes told her the depth of his feelings. A sting in her eyes announced her tears before they pooled and tumbled down her cheeks. Frozen, she stared as he flipped the box open and slid the sparkling diamond ring onto her trembling finger.

At last, as he stood and wrapped his strong arms around her and she huddled in the security of his embrace, she gave him the answer he sought.

"Yes."

And he kissed her in a wordless promise of forever.

ACKNOWLEDGMENTS

Thanks to my great team of ARC and beta readers, especially Tamie Dearen's Remarkable Romance Readers! You are awesome! Thank you: Wanda Liendro, Dana McCall Michael, Nadine Peterse-Vrijhof, Trudy Dapprich, Jessica Dismukes, Margie Shoemaker Harris, Clare Rauch Drexel, Loriann Peterson Merritt, Rennae McIntosh, Patti Ferrin, and Melissa Ann Medell Hayford.

Thank you to the Sage Vally Ranch authors, Bree Livingston, Melanie Snitker, Liwen Ho, and Crystal Walton! You are amazing authors and so wonderful to work with.

Thanks to my fabulous editor, Laurie Penner.

Thanks to my family and friends who put up with my stress and crazy schedule.

And last, but not least, thank you, sweet hubby, for taking care of me and providing endless romantic inspiration. Without you, I would have nothing to write!

ALSO BY TAMIE DEAREN

Sweet Romance

The Best Girls Series:

The Best is Yet to Come

Her Best Match

Best Dating Rules

Best Foot Forward

Best Laid Plans

Best Intentions

Sweet Romance

A Rose in Bloom

Restoring Romance

Fall Into Romance Boxed Set

Sweet Inspirational Romance

The Billionaire's Secret Marriage

The Billionaire's Reckless Marriage

The Billionaire's Wayward Marriage (Coming soon)

Christian Romance

Noelle's Golden Christmas

Haley's Hangdog Holiday

Shara's Happy New-foundland Year

Holiday, Inc. Boxed Set

The Alora Series

YA/Fantasy

Alora: The Wander-Jewel

Alora: The Portal

Alora: The Maladorn Scroll

Subscribe to TamieDearen.com and get your free books!

Follow on Facebook: Tamie Dearen Author

Follow on Twitter: @TamieDearen